JOY RIDE

POWERTOOLS: HOT RIDES, BOOK #4

JAYNE RYLON

HAPPY ENDINGS PUBLISHING

Copyright © 2019 by Jayne Rylon

All rights reserved.

No part of this book may be reproduced or shared in any form or by any electronic or mechanical means—including email, file-sharing groups, and peer-to-peer programs—without written permission from the author, except for the use of brief quotations in a book review.

If you have purchased a copy of this ebook, thank you. I greatly appreciate knowing you would never illegally share your copy of this book. This is the polite way of me saying don't be a thieving asshole, please and thank you!

If you're reading this book and did not purchase it, or it was not purchased for your use only, then please purchase your own copy. Refer to the don't-be-a-thieving-asshole section above for clarification. :)

V2

eBook ISBN: 978-1-947093-07-2

Print ISBN: 978-1-947093-08-9

Cover Design by Jayne Rylon

Cover Image by Wander Aguiar

Editing by Mackenzie Walton

Proofreading by Fedora Chen

Formatting by Jayne Rylon

ABOUT THE BOOK

Sometimes the hardest thing to protect those you love from is yourself.

Walker and Dane are a team. Best friends doesn't even begin to cover what they are to each other. Nothing can break the bond they forged during their tumultuous teenaged years or strengthened during their time in the military.

Except Joy. Dane's first crush and Walker's step sister, Joy has always had the power to throw a wrench in their lives even if she never realized her own allure.

So when she shows up at Hot Rods motorcycle shop, a newborn in her arms, nine months after they slipped and slept with her before leaving town to prevent another mistake... They know life is about to change for whichever of them is the father of her baby as well as the man who's not as lucky.

Especially when they realize her father isn't about to let her live the life she wants without a fight. Because no matter their own misgivings, they'd never let anything happen to the woman they've both loved for more than a decade. After all, they left her to protect her...even if it was from themselves.

This is a standalone book in the Hot Rides series and includes an HEA with no cheating. The series is part of the greater universe where both the Powertools and Hot Rods books are also set, so you can visit with many of your previous favorite characters and see what they're up to now!

ADDITIONAL INFORMATION

Sign up for the Naughty News for contests, release updates, news, appearance information, sneak peek excerpts, reading-themed apparel deals, and more. www.jaynerylon.com/newsletter

Shop for autographed books, reading-themed apparel, goodies, and more www.jaynerylon.com/shop

A complete list of Jayne's books can be found at www.jaynerylon.com/books

1

Joy had never been in so much pain in her entire life.

She screamed. She writhed. She cursed God and the men who had done this to her.

Then she clenched her teeth as she fought another excruciating spasm despite the way her vision dimmed on the edges. Was this what it felt like when you were dying?

Thanks to her stepfather, she couldn't even go to a hospital. Instead, she had to suffer.

Just when Joy thought she couldn't bear a single moment more, the agony relented. The soft, calming voice of her midwife penetrated her dark thoughts as the woman crooned encouragement in her ear. "Almost there. Be strong for your daughter. You'll meet her soon."

Of course, Joy couldn't comprehend the specific words so much as the tone they were uttered in. Her mind kept panicking and her exhausted body had long ago resorted to functioning off of adrenaline and instinct. She sagged against the edge of the inflatable pool that was supposed to make for a peaceful birthing experience.

My ass.

If it wasn't for the baby she'd felt growing inside her for months now, even as her own love for the child blossomed, she would have given up. Let the blackness take her. Sometimes she wondered if it was smart to bring an innocent child into the world. Especially a daughter.

What if she ended up as powerless as Joy herself? No. She would find a way to give her child a better life. Maybe she could even improve her own in the process.

Joy hated the men who'd put her in this situation.

Her stepfather.

His dirty right-hand man, Clive.

And especially whichever of the two guys she'd slept with who'd been the one to get her pregnant before abandoning her…yet again.

Strike that. On general principle, she hated *both* of them, regardless of which had knocked her up.

Another contraction wrung her midsection as if her own body was calling her a liar. Hadn't it already proven she'd never be able to resist either of them?

Worse, she hated herself for falling in love with them both even though she'd known neither of them would stay. How much different would this moment in her life have been if Dane or Walker or both were here to hold her hand and promise everything would be okay?

Joy couldn't help it. She began to weep. Normally she would shut those tears down, refuse to shed them or acknowledge how deeply Walker and Dane's rejection had cut her, but right then she used the excuse of her physical pain to mask the impact of the far deeper emotional wounds she bore.

"No, no. You're doing fine. This should be it. You're going to birth her head this time. Ready?" The midwife helped Joy focus on what was important. The future, not the past.

The rest of her labor was a blur as pain threatened to blot out her elation. But in the end, when the midwife guided her into bed and handed Joy her precious baby, it was rapture that won out.

In that moment she knew...all of it had been worth it.

Every bit of discomfort—today and for years before— her heartbreak, and even being left behind by the two men she had always longed for. Every hurdle she'd cleared had brought her to this moment.

"I swear I will love you like no one has ever loved me," Joy promised as she traced her daughter's cheek with the tip of her index finger.

Her child would never have reason to doubt that.

And if she had to prove it by fighting for them both to survive, that's what she was going to do.

As soon as she took about a three-day nap.

"Rest now. I'll stay until you've recovered enough to care for her on your own." The midwife took a seat, smiling at both Joy and her baby as if she was proud of them. Joy wondered if that's what it would have been like to have a mother who gave a shit about her daughter instead of only herself.

She would never be selfish when it came to her baby.

"Thank you," Joy whispered, annoyed when her eyes fluttered closed, stealing the sight of her child from her.

"What's her name?" the midwife asked.

"Arden." Joy hadn't planned to say that, but when she pried her eyelids open for one more glimpse at the baby in her arms, she knew it was the right answer.

Now if only the rest of her problems were so easy to fix, she'd be set.

2

SIX WEEKS LATER

Joy beamed as she rocked Arden, who'd fallen asleep in her car carrier on the way home from her final post-natal visit. Sure, she'd wailed when she'd gotten her shots, but even that hadn't riled her for long. She'd taken it like a champ and now seemed as docile as a kitten instead of the ferocious mini-dragon she sometimes transformed into. Wonder where she'd gotten that temper from? Oops.

A soft chuckle fell from Joy's lips.

Despite how worried she had been for both the trip into town and the visit itself, the doctor had confirmed what she already knew: Arden was perfect.

The most insignificant things about her daughter could hold her spellbound—a simple smile, the hazel color of her eyes, how tiny and precious every one of her fingers were. In fact, everything about the past six weeks had been magical.

Alone, she'd bonded with her baby and had nearly forgotten about the world waiting outside their very temporary haven. They'd have to go soon; she'd probably stayed too long already. Joy finally felt strong enough to take on the challenge of finding a permanent place to raise her daughter and rebuild their lives.

Today, she'd only imagined she'd seen Clive once while she'd exposed Arden and herself long enough to visit the clinic. Even then, she'd gotten her heart rate under control before her hands turned clammy or her stomach revolted. When driving home, she'd barely looked in the rearview mirror a half dozen times more than necessary. Progress.

For the first time in Joy's life, she imagined what it might be like to be...content.

When days had turned into weeks and no one had broken down the cottage's door or dragged her back to her stepfather's house, she'd started to believe that maybe he didn't care about her defection as much as she'd feared he would. It didn't even hurt her feelings because it meant she and Arden might be free to start over and live their lives however they chose.

Though they might struggle, especially right at first, Joy could make the most of a little to build something that was hers and hers alone. Beholden to no one. Unfettered by the repercussions that stemmed from dabbling in the gray areas of the law and the unsavory players that operated in that space. Like her stepfather.

Joy took a deep breath and tipped her face upward, relaxed for a moment.

She should have known that couldn't last.

A triple rap echoed through the bungalow that had been her safe haven. Loud enough and insistent enough to startle the baby awake. Which of course meant that Arden began to cry and that those cries were going to turn to wails if Joy didn't do something to appease her daughter. Like pick her up or feed her or sing her a lullaby.

In truth, those tactics might not work and the diva part of Arden, which she'd certainly inherited from her father, would emerge.

Joy was going to murder whoever was out there disturbing their solitude.

She stormed to the door, only remembering that no one knew she was there right before she'd nearly ripped the thing off the hinges so she could bark at the intruder. At the last moment, she hesitated, her fear returning as Arden's cries grew more insistent in the background.

Shit.

No one had been by this old abandoned cottage in the entire time she'd been squatting in it. In fact, Dane had once told her that no one had been there in years until he and Walker had used it for some much-needed relaxation of their own immediately after leaving the service. Part of her had maybe even hoped that's where they'd gone when they'd defected from her stepfather's empire—and her— once and for all.

That's why she'd picked the place when she fled.

Not that she'd had a lot of options with Arden on the way and very little cash in her pocket. Still, there was no use in pretending she wasn't there when Arden made it obvious someone was home. So instead she peeked out the sidelight, then froze.

Clive.

How the fuck had he found her and what was he doing here now?

She wasn't going to give in to him without a hell of a fight. She'd come too far to go back.

Schooling her pulse to remain steady, Joy mentally

reviewed her preparations. She wasn't entirely ready yet, but she'd known this could happen. There was a duffle bag of emergency supplies in the trunk of the car at all times. She just had to get him to leave or be distracted long enough that she could grab Arden and put the escape plan into motion.

Where they would go next, she had no clue. It didn't matter as long as it wasn't with Clive.

"Come on, Joy." He spoke to her through the door as if he were an innocuous, rational human being. Something she knew to be an utter lie. Pure evil like him shouldn't even be within a mile of her innocent child. "I know you're in there. I spotted you in that piece of shit town and figured you had to be here. What were you doing at that doctor's office anyway? And whose baby is that? Open the door so we can talk."

Ah, shit. She'd concocted a million different stories, but in the end, she figured the truth might work the best to deter Clive. Make herself as undesirable as possible to him. Besides, he was persistent and nosey and a complete toady. He would at the very least tell her stepfather every last word of what he discovered today. So she might as well give him the message she needed passed along anyway.

It could be her only chance to extricate herself from their world for good.

Joy prayed she was making the right decision. She looked over her shoulder at Arden and knew her baby was worth the risk. After a deep, shaky breath, she opened the door.

"Your father has been worried sick about you." Clive leaned on the jamb as if he was harmless—a neighbor dropping by to shoot the shit instead of a henchman who could drag her back to an existence she didn't approve of and punish her for daring to break the rules. She didn't miss how he positioned his body in the path of the door to prevent her from shutting it again.

"Angus is not my father," Joy snarled. Now that she was a parent herself, she couldn't see how the man who'd married her mother and ruled them like a ruthless dictator could ever be called that.

"He's obsessed with finding you and making sure you're safe." Clive cleared his throat, as if even he couldn't stomach that lie. "It looks bad on him that he doesn't know where you went. You know he can't have that. He counts on his reputation to keep people in line. There's talk that maybe his enemies got to you and that makes him seem weak. He's furious."

"Now *that* I believe." Angus was the president of Wildfire, an outlaw motorcycle club that was mostly a front for lucrative, if primarily illegal and always shady, dealings. He'd stayed on top all these years by being ruthless and never letting anyone circumvent his authority. Joy and her mother—who had foolishly married the bastard—included.

Fear was the main instrument he used to ensure compliance. While her mother had been willing to trade her independence for a twisted form of security, Joy was not. No longer. She stood straighter, clenching her fists. "And you're going to return me to him and reap the rewards. Am I right?"

"Think about this, Joy. How are you going to support yourself and a baby on the couple thousand bucks you stole from me? Which, by the way, you could have just asked me for. Money is nothing; there's plenty of it around. You know I'd have given it to you. I owe you that at least." Clive leaned in as if he was going to hold her hand.

She snatched it away before he could try. And yeah, he done more damage to her than that covered. She didn't even feel bad about the cash she'd swiped on her way out of town.

Joy prepared to employ the self-defense tactics she'd learned in her lessons from Walker and Dane. Too bad she hadn't been able to shield her squishy heart from them as well as she knew how to guard her body. "I don't know how I'm going to get by yet, but I'll figure it out."

"Did you come here hoping for protection from Walker and Dane? Are they here?" Clive licked his lips as he peered around her. He damn well better be nervous about that prospect. They hated Clive even more than she did.

"They're around," she lied.

"Is the baby Walker's?" Clive raised a brow. "That would be a hell of a game changer. The only person your father would love to have back more than you is him and if his son had an heir for Wildfire…"

Joy honestly couldn't say, because she didn't know for sure. Shame washed over her, goading her to lash out twice as hard. "Don't you fucking talk about my baby. Don't even think about her or who her father is. Just forget you saw anything and get out of here. Leave us alone and go home, Clive. With Walker, Dane, and me out of the picture, you can have what you always wanted. To take over after *that man* is dead. If you're really lucky, one of the rival clubs will off him sooner rather than later."

She refused to ever call Angus her father—step or otherwise—ever again.

To her surprise, Clive actually considered her words.

Walker and Dane had been a massive roadblock on his path to success. But she could tell the moment he thought of an even better solution.

A slimy grin spread across his face before he made her an offer she could absolutely refuse. "Come back with me, Joy. As my wife. We could say we eloped when we found out you were pregnant and that you wanted some time to yourself with the baby. I'll take care of you. I'll raise your child as my own. Give you everything you could want. You would be treasured. Spoiled, even. With you by my side and that tie to his family, you're right—your father would finally acknowledge me as his successor."

"Never!" Joy had to resist the urge to slam the door in his face.

No. That was not an option.

She was glad she hadn't had lunch yet or she might have lost it then. Even if it wasn't for what he'd done to her, all those years ago...

No. Hell, no.

Joy stumbled backward, swinging the door shut despite Clive's intrusion into the space.

He shoved it open again and took a step inside. "Even after all this time, you'd still choose one of them over me? They may have you now, but we both know who had you first. You'd rather fuck your own brother than sleep with me?"

"*Step*brother," she corrected. Walker, Dane, hell... anyone. Yes, she'd choose *anyone* else over Clive—the man who'd stolen her virginity and ruined her chances at a real relationship with either of the two men she'd adored since she was a kid.

Joy didn't have to say it. When she met Clive's questioning stare, it had to be plain.

He grimaced but, shockingly, nodded. "Fine, have it your way."

"What do you mean?" She narrowed her eyes, unwilling to trust his seeming change of heart.

"You're right. Knowing Walker and Dane are gone for good is enough. If you swear never to come back with their crotch fruit, who might give them reason to return someday, I'll cover for you." Clive acted like he was doing her a favor when she was practically clearing the way for all his disgusting dreams to come true.

If he was under the misconception that having her or Arden around Wildfire would entice Walker, she wasn't about to correct him. Neither Walker nor Dane gave a fuck about her. They were never going to get involved in Angus's bullshit empire again. But suddenly it didn't matter, because neither was she, as long as she could get the hell past Clive and run for it.

"Great. Have a good life. I've got to go." Joy turned her back on Clive, trusting that his ambition would hold and keep her safe by default.

"Are you meeting them in Middletown?" Clive wondered, though why he cared she couldn't say. "We heard they took jobs at a shop there."

"None of your business, remember?" Apparently none of hers either. She had no earthly idea where the pair of them were since they hadn't bothered to so much as send her a damn email after they'd fucked her then disappeared. And even if she knew, would she go to them?

Damn it. What choice did she have?

Joy just hoped she wasn't trading one tyrant for two more now that she had a destination in mind. She threw bottles of breast milk into her baby bag and gathered the bare essentials before scooping up Arden, still in her carrier.

Without hesitation, she stormed past Clive and to her car, where she took care to secure Arden in correctly despite her trembling hands.

Clive wandered over. She didn't want to give him time to reconsider, so she hurried.

"Watch your back, Joy," Clive murmured from behind her. "Not only will you be a target for your father's retrieval efforts, but you also won't have my protection or Wildfire's anymore. His enemies, and there are a fuck ton of them, are your enemies too. They certainly won't be interested in taking care of you, like I have."

"You know, Clive, your *protection* is something I'll be much better off without." Joy dared him to deny it as she shut the rear door of the car and climbed into the driver's seat. Clive held the edge of it in his fist, keeping her from peeling out of the driveway and getting as far away from him as possible.

Toward Middletown. She had no idea where that was, but she was about to find out.

He grimaced, his face redder than usual. "Staking a claim on you made a hell of a lot of other men, less civilized ones than me, back away. You're welcome."

"Fuck you." If he'd been standing in front of the car, she might have run him over right then.

"Be careful. That's all I'm saying." Clive winced. "I know you don't believe me, but I don't want to see anything bad happen to you."

"You don't think Walker and Dane can keep me and Arden safe?" He must be crazier than she thought. Of course they *could*. But would they? Or would they send her away since they obviously didn't want to be found either?

She just needed a chance to get on her feet and then she'd leave them alone. The last thing she wanted was to be owned by the pair of them instead of Angus and Clive.

Joy started the car and gripped the wheel. She could do this. She had to.

"They didn't last time, did they?" Clive taunted, allowing a hint of his true self to emerge. "Fine. Have it your way, Joy. Stubborn and prideful as ever. But you better hurry. I already called your father. He'll be here within the hour. And I won't be as gracious when you fail at this scheme of yours and wind up back at home. With me. Where you know you're meant to be. Then we'll do things my way."

Her snarl must have been vicious enough to upset Arden, who began to cry even louder.

"Sometimes I wish things could have been different." Clive reached out and touched her cheek with one finger, making her skin crawl.

It would be so much easier if she could give in. Believe him. Stay embroiled in the only life she'd ever known, both dicey and unfulfilling.

For Arden, she had to do better. They both deserved more.

Joy grabbed the door handle and yanked. Clive barely retracted his arm before she smashed it.

Then she took off, leaving him in her dust.

3

Walker couldn't sleep.

He paced the floor but couldn't get very far. They didn't call this a tiny home for nothing. He wasn't bashing it, though. He was grateful for a place of his own. Well, a place he could share with Dane, which was pretty much the same thing. They'd been living together since their military days and Dane had spent so much time at Walker's house when they were in high school, he might as well count that era too.

Walker didn't blame the guy. Dane had been infatuated with Walker's stepsister, Joy, and used their friendship to spend every second possible ogling her. If Walker said he hadn't appreciated the excuse to see more of her himself, he'd be lying. But that had been before everything went to shit...the first time.

It had taken a long, winding road to get them here, to the moment in time where they were doing what they loved—working on custom motorcycles—and being paid well for it.

Hell, the house had been an unexpected, but very appreciated, bonus. The fact that it was becoming somewhere to call home, well, that was even more incredible.

Walker and Dane had both been onboard with getting dirty and building it themselves, with help from their new employers and their friends. The Hot Rides motorcycle shop family was certainly a big one. Especially once you counted the gang from their sister-shop Hot Rods down the road and their construction worker pals, the Powertools crew, who were in town for an extended holiday vacation.

So why was he suddenly so anxious he couldn't seem to calm his mind long enough to enjoy his big soft bed and the quiet of the woods surrounding their new place?

Walker groaned and ran his fingers over his beard, shaping it the way he liked.

He knew exactly what the problem was. He just didn't want to admit it. Even to himself.

Spending every day around people in committed, blissfully happy ménage relationships was reminding him of what he and Dane had walked away from. It had seemed like the right thing to do at the time, but...what if they'd made a mistake?

A terrible mistake.

No. Walker shook his head in the dark. They'd done what was best no matter how much it had hurt them both. He paced to the wall separating his room from Dane's and put his hand on the freshly painted shiplap.

Dropping his forehead to the boards, he cursed the fact that he and Dane didn't have an excuse to share a space anymore. At least when they'd been living out of a hotel room, he'd been able to ground himself by watching his partner sleep. Counting Dane's deep breaths had sometimes even allowed Walker to drift off himself.

Now, all he could see in the black of night was the expression that had crossed Joy's face as she'd come around him and Dane the time they'd shared her. Who'd have thought she could take them like that, holding each of them so perfectly within her?

It had been the best, and worst, moment of his life. Because even as he'd relished her surrender and done everything in his power to enhance her pleasure, he knew that they were going to disappoint her come morning.

Again.

It was the last thing he'd ever wanted and the one thing he seemed best at.

Even now, he couldn't deny that he ached to do it again. His cock roused as he tried to scrub the memories of making love to his stepsister from his mind. Tried and failed, horribly.

Walker growled as he stalked to the wooden chair beside his bed and sank onto it. At least he slept naked, so he didn't have to waste time stripping off his pajamas to take matters into his own hands.

Literally.

He grabbed his cock, angry at himself that this was what it took to calm his mind and his body. It always came back to her and the one thing he couldn't have. So why couldn't he let it go?

Her. He couldn't let *her* go. At least not in his dreams.

Walker caressed himself as he remembered what it had been like, that night when they'd finally given in to the desire that had first awakened between them so many years ago. When Joy had barely been a woman and they were living in the same house, their parents recently married.

Dane had developed a crush on her from the first moment he met her. He and Walker had been best friends, even in high school, and the day Dane had been introduced to Walker's future stepsister, their lives had changed forever. If only things hadn't gotten fucked up, Walker was sure that Dane would have married Joy and lived happily ever after. But shit like that was only for fairy tales.

Instead, everything had gone to hell and they'd joined the military, getting shipped out before they could cross any lines, like killing Wildfire's sergeant-at-arms, Clive, and either pissing off his father for wasting one of his assets or going to prison for the rest of their lives because of it.

While they were away, their friendship had deepened into something more. Something intimate and...carnal. Only they could understand what the other had been through. But that hadn't stopped them from taking Joy when they were grown ass men who should have known better.

After they'd left the service, they didn't have anywhere to go. Aimless and unadjusted to normal life, they'd listened to Walker's father, who told them they'd always have a spot in his "organization". Except they quickly realized that wasn't going to work out either.

Both because of their disagreements with his good old dad, the asshole's unscrupulous methods, and his degrading morals. What had seemed like petty mischief when Walker left, had escalated to full-out criminal activity by the time he'd returned.

Oh, and also because of Joy.

It had been difficult to leave her alone as kids, when they didn't know how to seduce a woman properly or how to harness their own unconventional sexualities. These days...well, it had been nearly impossible not to take advantage of the one person they shouldn't have tarnished with their touch.

Joy.

She was even more beautiful now than she'd been years ago. Vulnerable, too.

Every day had been torture, spent so close to her while they tried to behave like something other than the savages they were.

And that one night, when things had gotten out of control, she'd showed them just how gloriously bold and sensual she could be despite the fact that they'd dragged her down to their level.

Walker cupped his balls and began to stroke his cock as he recalled the naughty smile she'd flashed him as he'd barged in on her getting out of the shower. Naked. Still damp. Her skin glistening as steam swirled around her.

And next thing he'd known, he'd crossed the room and started kissing the shit out of her.

Until Dane had stumbled across them, not seconds later.

Instead of closing the door or ripping Walker a new asshole, he'd joined them instead.

What they'd done with countless women had seemed so different when they'd shared it with Joy. It had been everything to him. And still not worth risking her place in his father's household. Her security. Her sheltered life.

What could they offer her instead?

Two hard cocks and a few minutes of fun?

Not worth it.

That hadn't stopped them that night, though. Once Walker had gotten a taste of her, he hadn't been able to force himself to stop until he'd devoured every last bite of her.

His fist moved faster as he remembered how he'd ordered Dane to go down on her while he studied every moan and gasp she'd uttered. How her nipples had darkened and hardened fascinated him.

And the way she'd opened her legs to him, even while still vibrating from the force of the orgasm Dane had given her, had rocked him. She'd welcomed him inside, held him close, and thrilled him by coming apart around him again and again.

Poor Dane hadn't been able to stand it either. He'd needed to be part of it, and when he'd taken a turn, sliding inside, where Walker had so recently been, Joy had massaged him with the slick heat of her pussy. Over and over, they'd taken turns while she'd smothered them in warmth and acceptance and ecstasy.

Walker couldn't sit still. He dropped his head back, thumping it harder on the wall this time. Of course, he forgot that Dane was right there, trying to sleep on the other side of it. When he heard rustling and the creak of a floorboard they must not have nailed down quite right, he realized he was about to be busted.

He froze, the hand wrapped around his dick not nearly adequate to hide the raging erection emerging from the top of his fist.

Sure enough, Dane wandered into the open doorway and leaned against the jamb, crossing his feet at his ankles. When he spied Walker's predicament, he grinned.

"You want a hand with that?" Dane asked, raising one brow. His sexy, sleep-rumpled grin was one Walker could never resist.

"I'd rather a mouth...or an ass." Walker grunted as he spread his legs farther apart, his muscles flexing and thrusting his cock through his fist instinctively.

"You know where to find me, you know. I only moved into the room next door." Dane came closer and put his hand on Walker's shoulder. But it was a hell of a lot easier to fuck than it was to talk about the reasons why he couldn't seem to rest lately.

Walker wasn't a saint. Far from it, and he needed what Dane was offering.

So he wrapped his arm around Dane's waist and yanked, dragging the other man into his lap. The chair he was sitting in tipped precariously before thumping back onto the floor, wooden legs banging against the planks. With Dane, he didn't have to worry about being gentle. The other guy could handle him, all of him, even these desperate, ugly parts.

He'd seen Walker at his worst and hadn't left him. Ever.

"It's bad tonight, huh?" Dane asked. The lines on his forehead that appeared when he was concerned prodded Walker to kiss him. It was better to shut him up before they had to discuss their issues. They could fix it the only way he knew how.

Walker reached up and framed Dane's face, bringing it to his own. He hoped the collision of their lips made up for his rough handling.

As always, Dane took what Walker gave him and defused it, made it into something beautiful and sensual instead of vicious. He reflected all that passion right back at Walker and gave as good as he got. When he raked his teeth over Walker's lower lip, something in Walker broke loose.

He stood, knocking Dane off balance, half-carrying him and half-shoving him until they tumbled onto his bed together. Walker lifted up just enough to lunge for his side table and the bottle of lube inside it. There was no pretending they were going to stop short of what they both craved. Not tonight.

Dane squirmed until he could roll onto his knees, his face down and his ass in the air. Walker slapped it, hard enough to make his open palm sting. "Did I tell you to do that?"

"No, sir." He quickly flipped over so he was flat on his back, waiting for Walker's next command.

"That's better. I want you this way, face to face." So it was impossible to forget who he was with and hopefully to erase Joy's ghost from his fantasy.

Walker hooked his hand beneath one of Dane's knees and lifted until he was open to Walker's advance. Then he grabbed the lube and slathered some on Dane's hot hole before giving his dick a thick coating too. He wasn't feeling especially patient and the last thing he wanted was to injure his partner.

Although he feared he already had in other, more complicated, ways.

Walker relished the seconds where his troubled thoughts receded and pure pleasure replaced them, taking up the empty room in his mind. He fit the tip of his cock to Dane's ass, then fisted the guy's hard-on as he pressed inward, connecting them once again.

The first few inches he fed Dane made both of them

shout with the intensity of the sensations bombarding them.

Dane put his hand up, caressing Walker's chest and then his abs, promising with that single touch that he was onboard, ready for more. He would take everything Walker could give him and then some.

Walker didn't deserve that kind of loyalty, but he would accept it anyway because he was a shitty, selfish person.

He slid deeper, working his way in until he bottomed out in Dane's ass.

Dane groaned and reached for his own erection, but Walker shoved his hand away so he could do the honors instead. He wrapped his fingers around Dane's long dick and stroked it, matching the pace of his pumping to the glides of his hips, fucking Dane inside and outside simultaneously.

"Fuck. It's been a while since we did this. I'm not going to last long." Dane scrunched his eyes closed before opening them, piercing Walker with his stare. "Do it. Fuck me. Hard and fast, like I like it."

"Like *we* like it." Walker needed Dane to understand that he got off on this just as much as his friend. It wasn't like he was doing this as some kind of sick favor or because the other guy was a convenient hole to bang.

He was a jerk, but he wasn't that cold.

Walker leaned forward and sank his teeth into Dane's shoulder. They'd been through some shit together and had a bond he thought was unbreakable. That didn't mean he planned to test that theory any time soon. If he scared Dane off, he'd have officially lost everyone he'd ever cared about.

Dane's arms came around Walker, holding him tight,

grounding him as he began to thrust in earnest. Dane rocked his hips up to meet Walker, making him sure that Dane welcomed every plunge of his cock.

With that assurance, Walker did his best to satisfy them both. He rode Dane, burying himself as completely as he could in the other man's body, connecting them as tightly as possible. And when Dane shuddered beneath him, he knew they were both riding a razor's edge of pleasure too intense to go on forever.

"Yes. *Yes.*" Dane dug his fingers into Walker's shoulders. The minor pain spurred him on. "Like that. Just like that. Don't stop."

If he didn't, he was going to tip over into bliss.

Walker didn't care. Because he knew that Dane would join him there in that place where all thinking stopped and only feeling existed.

He charged ahead, his pelvis smacking Dane's ass hard enough that the other man scooted up the bed until his head was at an awkward angle against the wall. Neither of them stopped.

Dane's ass got even tighter on Walker's cock, if that was possible, as his entire body gathered in preparation for his orgasm. Walker knew just the way to trigger it too.

He let himself fall first.

Walker fucked Dane with a flurry of movement that surprised himself. He pounded into his partner, grateful to be paired with someone who loved it every bit as much as he did when they got out of control like this. This was a side of himself he could never show to Joy.

Joy.

Shit. Not now.

But once he thought of her, he couldn't keep his imagination from running wild. His entire body jerked as the stray thought propelled him into climax. And as come blasted from his cock, filling Dane, all Walker could think of was the night Joy had been between them as all three of them had reached this peak—no, one even higher—together.

Dane spasmed then too, as Walker's hot seed washed over him. His cock jerked in Walker's fist a moment before he made a mess of his chest and abdomen with his own powerful release.

Walker rubbed him with the long, languid strokes Dane preferred when he came, drawing out the rapture for as long as he could, while still jabbing into Dane's ass with short plunges that bottomed him out in the other man.

And after their climaxes passed, he finally relaxed, smothering Dane, who didn't seem to mind.

When they could think and breathe again, Dane asked, "Did you just call me Joy?"

"Hell no. You must be hearing things." Walker grunted as he withdrew from the sanctuary of Dane's body and turned away, rolling to his side so he faced the wall and not his best friend.

"I miss her too, Walker. Bad." He put his hand on Walker's shoulder and squeezed. "Maybe we should email her. Invite her out to visit now that we're settled. Smooth things over. The way we left—"

"Was the way it had to be. Nothing's changed, and I can't say goodbye again. It would kill me." Walker buried his face in his pillow, refusing to look Dane in the eye even though he knew it made him a coward of the worst sort.

Dane sighed then and climbed from Walker's bed, leaving him utterly alone. "Yeah. You're right. Me too."

Neither of them slept the rest of the night, the things

they'd done becoming a wedge that drove them apart. Instead they tossed and turned on opposite sides of the wall between them, which could never be as divisive as the ones they'd constructed in their hearts.

4

Dane stared at Walker, his jaw hanging open. Had he heard his best friend correctly?

They were surrounded by friends so tight they seemed more like family than any of the blood relatives the two of them had ever known. The connections between the Hot Rides, Hot Rods, and Powertools crews reminded him of the one he and Walker had formed in high school and strengthened during their time overseas. The shit they'd gone through had made it impossible to tear them apart.

Yet somehow the two of them had been included in this gathering, welcomed with open arms to the celebration of a new year. A new life too for most of the Hot Rides, who'd had a hell of a time lately, fighting for their soulmates and earning some damn peace.

Dane could relate to that aspect at least. Stability, honest work, and a network of kind and kickass people—well, those were greater gifts than he'd ever expected to receive this holiday season.

He was beyond grateful. Swear to God he was.

With their immediate needs taken care of, though, old cravings had resurged. For him and he could tell for Walker, too. They had so much, yet no one special to share it with. And the one person they'd always wished had all these things they now possessed, they'd left behind. In the clutches of two men neither of them respected any more than they did themselves.

Here they were, on New Year's Eve, partying in the Hot Rides garage and contemplating even more new beginnings. That's when Walker had dropped his bomb, proving that their brains often thought just alike. "Maybe we need to try something different this year."

"Like what?"

"How about a serious relationship?" Walker asked, nonchalantly, as his stare tracked Kyra, Ollie, and Van across the impromptu dance floor they'd fashioned out of the Hot Rides garage bays. The trio was so fucking happy it almost hurt to look at them.

For years, Walker had insisted that their liaisons with women be limited to a single night of multiple orgasms. It was the best policy when the two of them were unreliable at best and dangerous at worst. Seeing Trevon, Quinn, and Devra along with Wren, Jordan, and Kason and now Van, Kyra, and Ollie all making their complex poly relationships work...

Well, Dane was starting to wonder if they might be able to do better—*be* better. So that they deserved that kind of love and could give it back tenfold.

If Walker was ready to commit to a relationship, especially a permanent ménage, then Hot Rides had really been a miracle for them. A place where they belonged and could openly pursue their most intense desires without repercussions or shame.

That sort of acceptance and understanding was having an enormous positive impact on them both. It was changing them.

But was it too late?

Dane recalled Joy's angelic visage and how she'd looked after they'd made love to her before slipping out into the darkness. There had been no going back, and still wasn't. But he would regret it for the rest of his life. Not the night itself, but the aftermath and all the things that had come before to make them unworthy of her love despite having stolen a taste of her body.

Walker was still staring at him. Waiting for a response. Hell, he had to know Dane was hungry for what he was proposing. Dane scratched the scruff on his cheek, wondering if he was understanding correctly. Afraid to hope only to be disillusioned again. "You mean, each of us with a woman by ourselves or one where we share someone together but for more than a night? Something like what they all have."

"Either, I guess." Walker shrugged as if it wasn't a big deal. Except to Dane it was. Those two things were entirely different. And if he had to sacrifice Walker to gain a girlfriend...frankly, he wasn't interested. He couldn't give up the one constant he'd had. Not now that things were finally looking up. "But if I have a choice...I vote for together."

"You have someone in mind?" Dane asked, focusing hard on Walker's eyes. His best friend didn't have any tells really, but Dane knew this man better than any other. And he could see it when Walker didn't deny what they both longed for.

Holy shit.

Dane considered whipping his phone out right then

and texting Joy to see what she was up to and if she hated their guts as much as she should.

Except he didn't have to.

Tom—the honorary patriarch of their newfound family and actual father of Eli, who himself was the head of Hot Rods—strode into the garage from the office, where he'd gone to see who'd pulled into the driveway. With a grim expression, he cut the music. Tom slapped his palm on the garage door button. As it rose, bit by bit, a very shapely, very familiar pair of legs came into view, followed by the very person Dane had been thinking of moments earlier.

What. The. Fuck.

"Hey, Walker. Is that Joy?" Dane shot to his feet, scrubbing his eyes as if she was some sort of mirage. Hell, he thought he saw her in every crowd, his soul longing for it to be true even when it wasn't. But no, she was as real and gorgeous as ever. Not in a traditional way; her features were too bold for that. But something about the sharpness of her nose and the angles of her jaw drew him to her inner strength.

Dane would know that auburn hair and no-longer innocent, still-nervous smile anywhere. His cock never got this hard this fast for anyone else. It was her all right.

Instead of answering Dane, Walker asked, "Why the hell is she carrying a baby?"

What? He tore his gaze from her breasts, covered by a soft, fuzzy sweater, to the tiny bundle she was carrying.

"Oh, shit." Dane's eyes nearly bugged out of his head. He glanced over his shoulder at Walker before rushing from the rear of the garage toward the door to take in Joy and—if his mental math was correct—a child that belonged to either him or his best friend out of the cold.

He'd played by Walker's rules last time. They'd only spent one night with her before moving on, but apparently those priceless hours would change him in more ways than they already had, ruining him for other flings.

Dane figured it probably made him a bastard to admit that part of him cheered at the realization that either he or Walker was going to be tied to Joy for the rest of their lives. He only hoped their friendship could survive considering they had both been in love with her for years, despite the fact that neither of them was good enough for her.

Walker didn't budge though he muttered a sardonic toast, "Here's to new beginnings."

Dane hissed over his shoulder, "Come on."

"You go." Walker hesitated, so very unlike him when he was around anyone but Joy, who'd always been his kryptonite. "It can't be me. I'm her goddamned stepbrother. How would that look?"

"Like you're not leaving a woman you care about and her infant out in the cold. Like you're not a piece-of-shit deadbeat if that child turns out to be yours." Dane refused to leave Joy hanging another moment. As it was, she was looking back and forth between him and Walker and then at all the other people gathered there—who'd pretty much all turned to stare at the unfamiliar face in their midst—as though she might bolt right into the frigid, inky night.

Alone. Cold. And scared.

Dane could read her fear in the stubborn tilt of her head that meant she was drawing on pure bravado. As always, it turned him on to see her in fight mode, though he wished she hadn't needed to don her imaginary armor so often in her past. Especially that one time…

When he'd failed her.

Dane lurched to a stop.

Would Joy even want him to be involved with her child when he hadn't been able to keep her safe? When he'd let her down so miserably?

No, she would prefer Walker. Always had even if she'd tried to hide her attraction.

In that moment, all of the circumstances and objections that had spurred Walker and Dane to leave her reared up and kept them apart. Their hesitation nearly cost them everything.

Joy saw both of them frozen in place and turned to Tom. "I'm sorry. This was a bad idea. I'm going to go…"

"Like hell you are." Amber—the wife of the Hot Rides garage owner, Gavyn—inched toward Joy, one hand resting on her own very pronounced baby bump while the other was outstretched toward their party crasher. "Forgive me if I say you look exhausted. I couldn't sleep tonight if you left on these pitch-black winter roads with that tiny baby. Please, come in. Let's shut these doors and warm you both up. Even if you're okay, your…"

"Daughter," Joy said as she pulled a blanket away from the baby's face and smiled softly. Her maternal affection, something none of them had experienced, was the most moving thing Dane had ever laid his eyes on. His chest ached as he watched Joy studying her child with such pride and awe. There was no doubt the baby was hers either. Joy's possessive grip said it plain enough. Though even if it hadn't, the shape of the infant's eyes, the color of her hair… All Joy. "Her name is Arden."

Dane stutter-stepped at the name. He looked again

at Walker, in time to see his best friend stagger then hunch over as if he'd been punched in the gut. Apparently he too remembered the random conversation they'd had one summer night, when he and Joy had been cuddled up watching a movie in Walker's room. Joy and Dane had tossed out some of their favorite names for their hypothetical future children when out of nowhere, Walker had said, "I've always liked the name Arden."

They'd teased him about it some...not because it wasn't a gorgeous name, but it was so unlike him to admit to having ever thought about a future that included a family of his own. That was the first clue Dane had gotten that Walker might be more than a little jealous of Dane's relationship with his stepsister.

While Dane—and apparently Walker too—concentrated on drawing a breath past his constricted chest, Amber came to the rescue.

"A beautiful name for an even more beautiful baby." She said with a thickness in her voice that meant she might cry. If anyone called her on her out-of-control hormones, she'd probably do some of that ass kicking she was capable of, even while about-to-pop pregnant. "She needs shelter even if you don't, okay? Please, come in out of the cold. You're welcome here. We take care of our own."

Several of the other people gathered around echoed Amber's invitation.

"I'm nobody's." Joy swallowed hard even as her gaze dropped.

Dane stood straighter at that and put a hand out toward her, though, like always, he was too far away to actually reach her.

"Somehow I don't think that's true," Amber murmured.

Joy looked between her and Walker, who nodded. Dane followed suit.

They sure as hell weren't about to send her away. At least not until they'd figured out what the fuck was going on and helped her however they could. Even if that meant keeping her away from them now that everything had shifted once more.

They'd have to keep themselves in check until then.

Her shoulders drooped a bit and she murmured, "Thank you."

Tom smiled at her and closed the door, shutting Joy in with them. Too far away to make it possible, Dane imagined he caught the sweet vanilla scent he associated with her. Then Tom turned the music back on, though lower, and shooed the rest of the crowd away to give them some space to get reacquainted.

While he did, Amber's mom and Tom's wife, Ms. Brown stepped in to take Joy under her wing. "Come on, honey. There's hot chocolate in the break room. My other daughter, Nola, has her two kids here tonight too. There are several others playing somewhere around. You seem new to this, but we're not. Let's get you settled and you can tell us what you need. We've got you covered."

Walker seemed as stunned as Dane, though they recovered enough to intercept Joy and Ms. Brown on the edge of the impromptu dance floor. He still had no idea what to say to her, though. So he stood there like an idiot, staring at Arden.

A baby. Joy's baby. Possibly *his* baby.

Holy fuck.

He should have said something, anything, to reassure

her, but it was hard to function when his mind had just exploded.

Joy's lower lip wobbled. If she broke, Dane would too. He couldn't believe they'd fucked up so badly and left her alone to deal with the repercussions of their single lust-filled night together. If he'd suspected before that he would never be worthy of her, he knew it for sure now. Doubly so when she glanced at Walker and him before double checking, "Is that okay?"

"We're not barbarians," Walker snapped as though he didn't believe it himself.

Joy flinched.

Dane glared at him.

Though Amber was tall and athletic, a gorgeous black woman who didn't take shit from anyone, she'd already broken through to the softer side of Joy. No simple feat; she didn't trust easily for good reason. "Forget your troubles for a little while, okay? It's New Year's Eve. The perfect time for a new beginning. You're among friends here, even if a couple of them are sometimes dumbasses and it seems like you have a bit of catching up to do. For the record, I've never seen them shut up this long. You must really have a hell of an effect on them."

Amber smacked Walker with the back of her hand in his gut, making him grunt. "Say something."

Walker sputtered then said, "Hi."

At least Joy cracked a smile at that. "Hey."

Dane's jaw felt like it was rusted shut, but at Amber's glare, he broke it loose. "Sorry, Joy. It's just a shock. Seeing you. And the baby. There's so much going through my mind right now I don't know where to start. Just come in, okay? Let's go into the break room where it's quieter so we can figure out the rest."

Joy's shoulders loosened and she relaxed her clutch on her daughter. Ignoring Walker and Dane for the moment, maybe because that was easier for her too, she asked Amber, "How far along are you?"

Together they escorted her to the back of the garage and into the common area where they'd shared so many meals and laughs over the better part of the year. Time Joy had obviously spent a lot differently.

Dane hated himself more than he ever had, which he'd thought impossible.

"Thirty-six weeks." Amber looked at Dane and Walker then, shooting them a glower every bit as stern as the comforting tone she was using on Joy. "I take it you know these boys?"

Joy snorted at that. "They're the biggest 'boys' I've ever seen. But yeah, you could say that."

"Right." Amber shut the break room door behind them, blocking out some of the revelry, then turned her attention to Walker and Dane. Dane appreciated her chaperoning to make sure they didn't fuck things up any worse than they already had. He suspected Joy might appreciate that too. "And you two want her to stay, don't you?"

"It's complicated, Amber." Walker scrubbed his hand over his beard.

"Yes." Dane said without thinking. Because it was true, even if it wasn't smart.

"Perfect." She smiled at him, encouraging him to do what seemed to be the right thing on the surface. "Well, they have a house here. It's not huge, but there's plenty of space for you and your daughter, even accounting for all the stuff that comes along with having a baby."

Joy grimaced. "What you see is pretty much what I've got. I kind of left in a hurry."

"No worries. I have a shit ton my friends gave us at my shower that I would love to share with you." Amber shared a wobbly smile with Joy. "This will be my first and I have no idea what the hell I'm doing. Some practice would do me good. Maybe we can figure out how to assemble and use some of this stuff together over the next couple of days if you hang around that long, huh?"

"That sounds incredible. So far I've been mostly winging it with the help of Google and then worrying I'm the worst mother in the history of the universe." Creases appeared between Joy's brows.

Dane extended his hand again. This time he brushed his fingers over her elbow, electricity running from the spot where they barely connected. "I've always thought you would be an amazing mother. I'm sure you *are* an incredible mom."

Joy shrugged away from his touch until they lost contact and some of the tension returned to her muscles, so he backed off.

Amber came to the rescue again. "Even if these two keep being idiots, as it seems they might have been, that doesn't mean you should leave if you don't have somewhere better to go, okay? Promise me. If you'd rather, I'll give you directions to a shelter Tom founded with his wife. Just come and get me at any time, okay? We live in the house you passed on the right as you came up the driveway to the shop."

"From what I could see, it looked really cute. The Santa on the motorcycle was a nice touch." Joy grinned, dazzling Dane with her smile. He was staring at her so hard, trying to soak in every last detail about her and the baby he still couldn't quite believe was real, that at first he didn't notice Walker was edging closer, about to burst with all the things they were both dying to know. "And I appreciate your offer, but that's probably not a good idea. There might be…people…looking for me."

"Amber, could we have some privacy, please?" Dane tried to keep his voice level and calm despite the flurry of emotions wringing his guts. Was Angus chasing her? Clive? All of Wildfire could be a few miles behind and ready to swarm Hot Rides.

They had to find out so they could warn everyone about the trouble they'd brought to Middletown if necessary.

Amber cut her gaze to Joy. "Up to you."

"Yeah. I gotta do it sometime. Might as well be now." She took shaky breath so deep her baby roused and blinked her eyes open. Dane was captivated. It was a real, miniature human being that was part Joy and part…

He couldn't even allow himself to think Arden might be part his. It could destroy him if he did. He'd given up on that dream forever ago.

With a few rubs on the baby's head, Joy resettled the child. Before leaving, Amber pointed at Walker and then Dane. "I like her. Don't chase her off or I'll be pissed. So will Wren and Jordan. You know they've been wanting a baby around here to spoil."

Dane couldn't help it. He smiled, even if it was faintly. Everyone loved Joy. Including them. That was the problem. "We'll do our best."

Amber softened her stern tone when she smothered first him and then Walker in a world-class hug. She whispered something in his best friend's ear before patting his cheek and leaving the break room, closing the door again behind her.

Outside, their friends began the countdown to New Year's en masse. *Ten...nine...*

Dane wasn't sure he felt like celebrating anymore. Dreaming about the future with Walker was one thing. Actually having it right there within reach and yet impossible to grab, well, that was enough to make him give up for good.

Three...two...one!

Muffled cheers, clapping, and shouts of, "Happy New Year," trickled into the awkward silence lingering between them. Dane could promise he wasn't going to forget this one any time soon.

Before he could think of something appropriate to break the ice with, Walker jumped right in. "How did you find us?" he wondered, his tone sharp.

If Joy had tracked them down, that probably meant Angus knew where they were too.

Shit. Dane had hoped they'd have a little more time to fly under the radar before they drew Wildfire's attention to Middletown. Now that they had gotten attached, it would be awfully hard to move on. In the few short months they'd been at the shop, they'd started to put down roots. Ones he suspected could go deep, if they were allowed to grow.

"Clive." Joy practically spit the bastard's name at them. Dane didn't blame her.

A memory reached out and slapped him back to the past. To their teenaged years. They'd come home late one night after he and Walker had gone to an end-of-summer bonfire, drank too many cheap beers, then stumbled back to Walker's house since Walker's parents wouldn't give a fuck if they were intoxicated. He'd sobered up pretty damn quick when he'd found Joy huddled in the corner on the floor of the bathroom, sobbing.

Her eye had been blackened and her clothes torn. Dried blood left a rusty stain on the inside of her pale thigh.

"Who the hell did this to you?" he'd shouted as his mind blanked out. It was rare that he lost his temper, but in that moment it had only been Walker's steady hand on his shoulder that kept him from murdering the person who'd harmed her—his innocent girlfriend, and his best friend's stepsister.

He'd refused to take Joy with them that night despite her begging, because he'd known the party would be too much for her. And look what had happened. It was his fucking fault she'd been left unsupervised with the bikers that always hung out at Walker's place, part of his father's motorcycle club.

It was his fault that she'd been abused. Raped.

Even now, he shuddered beneath the force of the rage that flooded him. At Clive, the older guy who belonged to the world he and Walker had only ever hovered on the fringes of. That bastard had claimed to be Joy's boyfriend for the next several years, and she had never denied it—not to Angus, Walker's father, not to the rest of the guys in the motorcycle gang, and certainly not to him or Walker. She had never again given Dane the honor of that designation after he'd left her alone and the unthinkable had happened.

After that all bets had been off.

Because being with Clive afforded her protection that being with Dane hadn't. It sheltered her from the rest of the thugs who hung around when he and Walker ran away from their problems. Dane had never resented her for failing to mention their dates and sweet kisses after he'd so obviously fucked up.

Mostly he was angry at himself.

How had he let that happen to her? All so that he and Walker could indulge in a few hours of meaningless fun.

They'd never recovered. Because every time he heard her screaming after one of her nightmares, or saw her flinch at one of his incidental touches, he knew he'd ruined the future for them both. He didn't blame her for not wanting him, or trusting him, after that.

A month later he and Walker had been approached by a recruiter. Together, they'd enlisted to make a difference in the world. To right some of the wrongs they'd been responsible for and escape the path they were on, which could only lead to darker deeds done for Walker's father in the name of Wildfire.

They left Joy the hell alone.

Dane had loved her with all his heart, but that hadn't been enough to make her happy or keep her safe. He wouldn't make that mistake again. Not now that he and Walker had complicated her life even further and left her carrying the weight of their poor decisions.

That didn't mean he wouldn't take care of her as best he could without involving his emotions, though. He stepped between her and Walker before his friend could launch a complete interrogation. The last thing he wanted was to scare her off. If she ran, she wouldn't even have what little security they could afford her. "It seems like you've had a rough few days. Can you jot down anything you might need so I can let Amber know, then we'll get you settled so you can rest. We can discuss this more in the morning."

"I'm still not sure…" Joy eyed the door.

Walker crossed his arms and spread his booted feet. Sometimes he was more like Angus than he would appreciate.

Joy rolled her eyes at him. "Settle down. I'll stay. But not because you bullied me into it."

It was obvious she didn't have many other options. Neither had they when they'd stumbled across the help-wanted ad for Hot Rides and practically begged for a job.

"No pressure." Dane said, despite every instinct that screamed at him to throw her over his shoulder and bolt her inside their house where they could keep an eye on her and her baby.

"Fine. Whatever. Let's go. As long as you have a bed, I'm in."

Both he and Walker went silent at that. Had it been anyone else at all, or any other time, Dane was sure one of them would have made a wisecrack about having a pretty woman in their bed. Thankfully, Walker kept his comments to himself and so did Dane.

The direction of their thoughts must have been apparent anyway. Or maybe Joy had the same idea. She blushed, then stammered, "I mean, for sleeping. By myself. Well, with Arden. No one is going to take her from me. Do you understand that?"

She stood tall then, turning her shoulder slightly as if to come between them and her daughter more quickly if needed.

Dane held his hands up, palms facing her. "That's not even a possibility. No one is thinking that."

"She's yours," Walker agreed, keeping Dane from having to deck him.

And finally, Joy relented. She wilted, sinking into a

chair at the table and nodding. "Okay. We'll stay. But only until I can get on my feet and provide for Arden on my own. That's all we need. That's all I'm asking of you."

Dane couldn't deny the knife that stabbed his heart then. Because he wanted to give her so much more. Always had. And just like before, he would never be able to. Too much had happened between them. Even the best mechanic had to admit when something was broken beyond repair.

Their New Year's resolution went up in smoke. It hadn't even lasted an hour.

Because if he couldn't have Joy, he didn't want anyone.

5

Walker paced the front porch of the tiny home he and Dane had built. The cornerstone of their foundation at Hot Rides. Unfortunately, it wasn't anywhere near big enough to contain the tension turning his muscles into pretzels. Which was why he'd spent the darkest stretch of the night freezing his balls off as he kept watch in case someone had followed Joy to their not-so-hidden hideout.

The first rays of sunrise pierced the glowing sky. It should have relieved him to see the breaking dawn, the start of the new year and new life he'd resolved to make the most of only hours before.

Walker should have known it was too damn easy when the very woman he craved had appeared before him as if his wicked thoughts had summoned her.

Of course there was some fucking wrinkle. Even more reasons—including a giant one in the form of a tiny, adorable human who hadn't asked to be entangled in their ongoing bullshit—why Joy still couldn't be theirs. A reminder that he wasn't destined to have simple pleasures like ordinary people. Hell, he'd be better off if he learned to quit hoping for them anymore.

Dane was inside. He'd stayed after helping Joy get settled into their space. Though Arden didn't seem to be a big fan of sleeping through the night, Walker had glimpsed Joy crashed out on their couch for several stretches while Dane had fawned over the exhausted woman.

Walker wished he could go in there and care for her, too, even though he knew that wasn't his place. Several times he'd gotten as far as laying his hand on the door knob before he remembered who he was and why Dane was much better suited to the role.

He should stay the fuck away from them. Let the universe reunite his best friend and his best friend's girl—Walker's own stepsister. Maybe Arden would bring them together, the way they always should have been. That baby had to be Dane's. Walker refused to ruin the lives of the three people who meant the most to him in the world. So what if he'd only met one of them a few hours ago? He refused to intrude on what could be a perfect, happy little family.

Walker rubbed his chest as if that would erase some of the pressure there.

At six on the dot, Walker's phone buzzed in his pocket. He withdrew it in time to see an unknown number flash across the screen. His eyes narrowed. He'd long ago blocked Angus from contacting him. That didn't mean the bastard didn't try to get around the ban. Often.

His father woke this time every morning. No doubt Clive had been there to suck his dick. Okay, not literally—probably—but he'd almost certainly had Joy tailed and reported their reunion to his pops.

It would never be finished. They would never escape entirely.

Just knowing his father was on the other end of the line, reaching one of his slimy tentacles out toward Middletown, made Walker want to hurl his cell across the yard into the woods beyond. So he stabbed the icon to disconnect the incoming call.

Less than ten seconds later, he got a text from the same number.

If nothing else, he'd inherited his stubbornness from his father.

The message read *How's Joy?*

Walker pinched the bridge of his nose before tapping out a reply. *Don't worry about her. I'm taking care of the situation.*

Joy had come to them. If nothing else, that meant she'd had enough of Angus and his God-complex, served with a side of oppression. Walker wasn't about to let his father dictate the situation any more than he already had.

Merry belated Christmas, son. And congratulations on one hell of a gift. Remember, you and your family—my family—always have a place here. This is where you belong.

Fuck that. Whether or not Joy's baby was also Walker's, there was no way in hell he was about to let either of them stay stuck under Angus's thumb. Unless that's what Joy wanted.

He froze, his booted foot clomping onto the deck boards.

What if she hadn't left on her own but had been ostracized instead?

Angus said they were welcome to return to their old life. But what if he would only take Joy if it was a package deal? Had Walker cost her a cushy existence? One where she was a prized possession, just like her mother had been before her?

Shit.

Walker stormed inside for answers. Ones he could trust. At least he could look Joy in the eye as he questioned her. Nothing Angus told him was reliable and he didn't want to give his father any additional advantage by admitting he had no idea what was going on.

Hell, he'd hardly recovered from the astonishment of seeing Joy with a baby and knowing there was a chance Arden could be his daughter too. He was terrified to even imagine the possibility only to have it snatched away again.

So he might have slapped open the door a little harder than he'd intended, sending it careening into the shiplap with a bang.

Of course that startled Arden, who began to scream.

"I just got her to sleep." Joy closed her eyes, her head tipping downward. She looked as if she might conk out mid-sentence.

"Here, let me." Dane held his hands out, waiting for Joy to place the baby into them. "I don't really know what I'm doing, but I can walk around with her like you did."

Joy smiled up at Dane then, riling Walker further as envy twisted deep within him like a coiling snake. He'd never been jealous of his best friend before. Not even when the guy had dated Joy so long ago. But seeing them together, with the child, made him realize that this was everything he'd ever wanted and would likely never have.

Joy. Dane. For them to be a family.

Carefully, Joy laid her daughter into the crook of Dane's arm, showing him how to support Arden's neck. She straightened the baby's teeny clothes and kissed her forehead. Seeing Joy hovering so close to Dane, and so affectionate, made Walker want to howl.

Instead, the questions that were building inside him broke loose, propelled by envy and wrath over everything he couldn't have. "What are you doing here, Joy?"

Her head snapped up and her gaze locked on his. "Same as you. Trying to survive."

"Angus said you're welcome home if I go with you. So tell me, did you run from him or did he kick you out so that you could lure us—*me*—back?" Walker gritted his teeth to keep from spitting out the other things he wished he could say.

"Wait, what?" Joy's chin wobbled as if he'd backhanded her. "You think I'm using Arden to manipulate you? Jesus, Walker. I know you don't have a very high opinion of me, but that's fucking nasty. Even for you."

"Is it true?" Walker asked again.

Dane stepped closer to Joy. "Cut it out, Walker. You know Joy would never fuck us over like that."

"Of course I wouldn't. But what about you?" Joy snarled, the poison in her tone at odds with the flash of resentment in her eyes. "You ratted me out to your father? Why would you tell him I'm here? Are you hoping he'll send Clive to pick me up so you can get back to your new life without any...complications?"

Walker didn't deny that sounded pretty heavenly right about then. Except for the fact that meant he'd have to give up Joy, and her daughter—this time forever. He shrugged one shoulder. "He sounded like he already knew where you were."

"You've been away from him and his tricks too long." She groaned. "He's going to make Clive try to convince me to do what he wants. Or worse, show up himself. I have to go. And you should too, if you're smart. He's been on a rampage ever since the two of you left. And I'm sure I haven't improved his mood."

"No." Walker spread his legs and crossed his arms.

"What do you mean, no?" Joy flailed, looking adorable despite her obvious distress. "It's not safe here. He didn't know I was pregnant. I hid it or he never would have let us out of his sights. You know how he is when he wants something. I won't be responsible for someone getting hurt. Not Arden or me, or you guys, or your coworkers and their families, who seem…incredible. I'm leaving."

She stood and began to cross toward Arden. Dane put his hand on her upper arm and squeezed. He angled slightly away from her to keep Arden resting on his arm, where she'd surprisingly drifted off again despite their raised voices. "Running isn't going to solve your problems."

"Really? You son of a bitch. You have a lot of nerve saying that to me after what you two pulled." She propped her hands on her hips.

Walker thought Dane should have taken some precautions because her knee wasn't too far from his best friend's balls and they'd made sure she knew how to use it.

"I'm sorry we bounced after making love to you," Dane murmured. The apology flew from his lips so steadily that Walker knew he'd been wanting to say those words for a long time. Pretty damn close to a year, he'd bet. "It seemed like the right thing to do at the time."

"And now?" She peered up at Dane with those doe eyes of hers, and Dane leaned in.

Walker didn't blame him. Joy was hard to say no to at

the best of times. Vulnerable and lost, she was irresistible. He would have done just about anything to erase the misery he saw in her eyes. So he didn't stop Dane when the guy inched nearer and prepared to kiss her unshed tears away.

"If you weren't holding Arden, I'd slap the shit out of you for that." Joy stepped backward so quickly that Dane tipped off balance. "Just because I had no other choice but to seek you two out for shelter doesn't mean I'm hoping to hook up with you again. Been there, done that, and have the baby to prove it."

"So she is…ours?" Walker felt odd even saying it.

"She's *mine*." Joy stood straighter then. "And no one—not Angus or Clive and certainly not either of you—will take her from me."

"No one's going to do that," Dane promised.

Hell, if his own father and Joy's mother had cared half as much about them as he could already see that Joy did about Arden, maybe they wouldn't be so fucked up they could hardly function as responsible adults themselves.

He owed it to Arden to make sure her mother and father—Dane—avoided making the same mistakes. Joy never had answered directly. It shouldn't matter, he reminded himself. Either way, he would shelter Joy and her daughter, make sure they were provided for.

"Dane's right, Joy. Hot Rides is a safe place. This is your best shot at breaking away from Angus, Clive, and Wildfire. Sure, my father knows where we are, but he can't do anything about it. These people are our family now. They could easily become yours too. Stay here and you'll be protected by us all, I swear it."

"Have you both lost your minds?" She shook her head.

"I'm not taking any chances with Arden. Get the hell out of my way."

"I've spent my entire life running from this mess, and for what?" Walker couldn't deny it any longer. This was his destiny. And until he faced his demons, they were going to continue to haunt him.

He looked over at Dane, who nodded slowly.

This time they had to stand and fight. For all of their sakes.

He'd go talk to Quinn, his boss, and Gavyn—Quinn's boss. Hell, to all the Hot Rides and Hot Rods, since they'd be subjected to Angus's ire if he, Dane, Joy, and Arden stayed. It was only fair. And if they asked him to leave, he would.

Angus had connections, especially in the biker world. He could make life difficult for the people who'd taken Walker and Dane in and made them feel at home. Physically, he wouldn't flinch at threatening them. Economically, he had some shady businessmen who could interfere with the shop and their livelihood wrapped around his dick. Angus would stop at nothing.

So Walker would accept it if Quinn told them to get out.

Somehow, though, he didn't think it would come to that.

The rest of the gang came from equally rough spots in the world. And yet they'd pulled themselves out of the shit they'd been dealt by sticking together. His gut said that meant they would stand with him.

No, he was sure of it. That certainty did something to him. It gave him an advantage he'd never had when dealing with Angus before. "It's going to be okay, Joy. I'm telling you, things are different now. None of us are kids anymore and Angus isn't the all-powerful puppet master he seemed while we were growing up. Dane and I are making this work on our own, and so can you."

"You have skills at least. You've been working on bikes since you were old enough to hold a wrench." Joy bit her lip then, casting her eyes toward the floor.

"It was really the only thing I liked about my father's club. That and riding, of course." He hadn't meant for that to sound so dirty, but looking at Joy and admitting it made his love for mounting both motorcycles and the women who hung around them apparent.

Thankfully, Joy didn't give him shit for speaking the truth.

"What am I going to do?" She slumped against the kitchen counter then. "I have nothing to offer. No money. No experience. How can I change the future for Arden and me?"

"You don't need to worry about that." Walker could at least give her this. "We'll take care of you. *Both* of you."

He expected her to be relieved, maybe even a little happy about the turn of events.

Nope, not Joy. She surprised him as always, making him wonder if he'd ever have a clue when it came to her and what she really needed.

"No. Hell no." Joy shook her head. "I'm not my mother. I won't be that kind of example for Arden. I can't be bought or kept. I'm my own woman and I'll make my own way. Somehow. I owe it to *my* daughter."

She probably didn't mean to trample Walker's own insecurities, but something about her refusal to admit what they all knew triggered him.

"Say it, Joy. Be honest. Whose baby is she?" Walker

asked, unable to stand the elephant in the room another moment.

He should have known better than to challenge her when she was pissed. She practically spat, "Maybe she's Clive's."

Walker didn't want to believe that was possible. Joy had been backed into a corner and was using whatever teeth she had to launch some sort of attack against him. And yet, the very idea stung him so badly he thought he might crash to the floor. He stumbled backward. The distance between them allowed him to see Dane's face and the shock and dread written in the creases there as he peered at the delicate new life in his arms.

They would love Arden because she was Joy's. But in that moment, Walker realized that both he and Dane had already also fallen in love with the idea that the baby could be theirs.

If Joy bolted and took Arden with her, they would lose everything.

He had to do everything in his power to keep the pair of them close.

And that made him just like his father.

Fuck my life.

6

Joy didn't know what had possessed her to fling such an obvious and hurtful lie in Walker's face, except maybe the desire to wound him as badly as he kept doing to her, even if inadvertently.

How dare he tell Angus where she was?

How could she trust him or Dane when they kept betraying her?

Now, last year, and a long time ago too.

It would have been nice to have even a single night where she didn't have to worry about that bastard or Clive coming to reclaim her—and her baby, who would become a trophy for both of those control freaks.

"You don't mean that, do you?" Dane asked quietly, careful not to rouse Arden. His tender care melted Joy's heart and her ire along with it.

"No." She shook her head. What people thought of her for her decision to sleep with both of these men—at once—was irrelevant. Especially because she wouldn't change it for the world. But she didn't want them to think she'd left their bed for Clive's either willingly or not.

Joy shrugged, attempting to let the shame and embarrassment roll off her shoulders along with so many other injustices. What was one more?

A lot. Because coming clean to Walker and Dane about her sexual history meant humiliating herself in front of the only two men she'd ever cared for or willingly allowed to possess her body. So what if it had been at the same damn time?

Joy loved them. Or she had.

At the moment she wasn't sure if the intense emotion inside her was more that or hate.

Funny how they could be so intertwined sometimes.

"What do you want me to say?" Joy asked. "That she's yours or that she's not, so you can go on about your life guilt-free?"

Arden was the best thing to ever happen to her. If they didn't see it the same way, then fuck them.

It was Walker who answered right away, catching her off guard. "I didn't know I wanted kids until I saw you walk through that garage door with her in your arms. But now I think it might kill me if you tell me she didn't come from that night we spent together."

"Say she's ours," Dane pleaded. "Yours, mine, and Walker's."

"Is that a thing?" Joy looked between the guys sheepishly.

"Technically, I suppose not." Dane held Arden close to his chest, rocking her as surely as if he'd been doing it for years. "But if she's mine or if she's Walker's, it feels better to me than if she's not either of ours at all. And hell, no matter who donated the sperm, I'm more than willing to step up. I'm tired of missing out. I don't want to do that anymore."

Joy Ride

"Me either." Joy looked up at Dane then. He'd always been her ideal partner. When they were teenagers he'd been her first love, until her feelings for Walker—the son of the man her mother had married—had confused her. And then Clive had ruined any chance of them figuring things out between the three of them.

None of them were able to function properly in the aftermath of that trauma.

She put her arms around Dane's waist, the gesture as familiar as if she'd done it ten minutes ago instead of ten years ago, and tucked in beside their daughter. It might have exposed her weakness, but she couldn't deny that she felt stronger by his side. "She's yours. One of yours. I haven't been with anyone else."

"Since the night we spent together, you mean?" Walker asked, a softness coming over his expression as he studied her resting in his best friend's embrace.

"Not ever. Unless you count the night Clive raped me. Which I definitely do not." She leaned into Dane when he clutched her to him tighter, his fingers digging into her hip.

Walker's jaw hung open. "Do you mean to say...?"

"Yeah, I was pretty much a born-again virgin until you two had your way with me then disappeared last winter." She shrugged, as if it meant nothing to her. Not the impact of Clive's attack or the fact that they had been able to overcome her massive inhibitions before taking off.

"I'm sorry, Joy. So sorry," Dane said in a rush. Whether he was apologizing for abandoning her recently, or for what had happened to her that summer night so long ago, or the varsity-level sexathon they'd engaged in despite her inexperience she wasn't sure. Probably all of the above. Though he'd had nothing to do with it, he'd always felt responsible for Clive's attack and the fact that they hadn't been home to stop it.

Beating the shit out of the guy was what had put Dane on the radar of the military recruiter in the first place. Angus had told the guy about Dane, what he'd done, and how he needed some discipline to harness his "aggressive" tendencies.

Of course it had all been bullshit. Dane would never harm someone without a good reason. And Angus had been threatened by the strength of Walker and Dane's friendship, even then. It made Walker way more difficult to mold into the perfect little Wildfire minion. So he'd hoped to get rid of him.

The fact that Dane had lost his cool over the things that had been done to her had both soothed her and made her feel guilty at the same time. It was because of her that he'd shipped out. Nobody, not herself and especially not Angus, had expected Walker to go with him when he left.

Walker had chosen Dane over her. Or maybe he'd simply needed to flee for his own sanity. More likely, though, he'd been compelled to protect his best friend and see him through that dark time.

In any case, that had been the first time she'd lost them.

Joy would never forget Dane's parting words to her that day. She'd told him, "Stay safe and come home soon."

To which he'd replied, "I hope I don't come back at all."

The desolation in his eyes had hurt her more than the physical damage Clive had inflicted. Because she realized then that Wildfire's sergeant-at-arms had destroyed more than her innocence that night. She'd lost everything she cared about.

Except years later, unexpectedly, they *had* come back. Briefly.

After hanging out in the cabin she'd given birth to Arden in for a few months, they'd given in to Angus's cajoling and returned home. They'd only stayed long enough to realize they didn't belong there any more than she did. And to get her pregnant before moving on. She was still too upset about that to ask why they hadn't at least taken her with them when they went.

Joy cleared her throat then, shaking all three of them from whatever memories they were each reliving. For her daughter, she would swallow her pride and beg if she had to.

"Guys, I've never asked you for anything. But I'm asking now. If Clive or Angus shows up, they can have me. I'll go back if it shuts them up and helps Angus save face among his associates, and his rivals, but...Arden... She needs to be free. Promise me you'll protect her, raise her to be her own woman, and let her flourish as she should." Joy broke loose of Dane's hold. Instead, she hugged herself, hoping to keep her roiling guts inside her body when even the possibility of being separated from her daughter made her feel as if she'd been eviscerated.

"I swear to you, Joy." Walker didn't hesitate. "I will keep your daughter safe. No matter what. I will not fail her."

He didn't say it, but she knew what he meant. He wouldn't let her down like he assumed he'd done to her. Walker took a step closer and then another, until they were definitely in each other's personal space. He smelled amazing, like the crisp forest night air. The heat radiating from him tempted her to bury her face against his powerful chest.

If they weren't careful, the chemistry they'd always shared would lead to more poor decisions.

Overwhelmed and confused, Joy wondered if she was doing the right thing. Did this seem like the best decision because it was or because being near them and becoming a family was everything she'd always desired?

It was her biggest fear—that she would turn out to be selfish, like her own mother had been. No, Joy swore to put Arden's needs ahead of her own. Today and every day for the rest of her life.

She laid her hands on Walker's chest and shoved until they broke a few steps apart.

If she licked her lips as she imagined what it would have been like to taste him again, no one could blame her, could they?

Dane groaned and spun away to stare out the window for a moment. The rapid rise and fall of his shoulders promised he wasn't unaffected either.

Joy scrubbed her eyes, then shoved her messy feelings down deep. She'd gotten good at compartmentalizing in order to keep going. Someday, that would probably come back to bite her in the ass, but for now it worked.

"It's time for Arden to eat." Joy changed the subject as she opened the fridge and took out one of the bottles she'd prepped during the middle of the night. "I'll take her, Dane."

He turned, a wince slashing across his face as if he didn't want to relinquish the baby just yet.

Joy knew how he felt. It calmed her to know that he was already under her daughter's spell.

"Teach me how to feed her?" he asked, making her heart do flip-flops in her chest.

It was simply about survival, she lied to herself. If something happened to her or if Angus found some twisted way to lure her back to his empire, the guys needed to know how to care for Arden.

Every instinct in her objected to the thought of leaving her child behind. But she would do whatever was best for Arden in the grand scheme of things. Even if that meant giving her to Walker and Dane to raise.

Arden looked even tinier than usual in Dane's strong yet tender grasp.

First she showed him how to heat the bottle in a warm water bath. Then she uncapped it and handed it to him, telling him everything he needed to know to provide nourishment for the baby. She even told him about the formula she had as a backup. In case she couldn't, or wasn't there, to provide sustenance for their child.

It felt good to be confident about what to do. To realize that she'd taught herself how to care for a whole new person. And when Dane did the same, he looked up at her with so much satisfaction and pride in his eyes, she knew he would make a perfect father. Even Walker took a half step closer, paying close attention to her instructions. With two dads like them, Arden might not need a mother.

She might not need Joy.

Especially with the support of the other wonderful people that seemed to congregate at the Hot Rides garage.

Joy accepted the truth. She might never have everything she desired from Walker and Dane, but she needed them because her daughter needed them. And she would do anything for Arden, even if it meant remaining so close to everything she'd ever desired without the possibility of actually attaining it.

"Okay. You guys win." She nodded. "I'll stay."

She just hoped she was doing it for the right reasons.

The *only* acceptable reason, that was. For Arden, and not for the parts of herself that would always be infatuated with both Dane and Walker.

"Good. Whatever happens, we're in this together," Walker assured her.

For now, she thought. For now.

Except this time it might be her who bailed when things got too difficult to bear.

7

Walker stepped outside, but even before he could shut the door, Dane was there, shoving through it onto the porch. He closed it firmly behind him, checking over his shoulder to make sure Joy wasn't about to follow suit.

"Where are you going?" Dane asked, putting one hand on Walker's arm.

He shrugged it off. "To talk to Quinn and make sure we can live up to all those promises we just made. They deserve to know what's going on, and if they ask us to leave, we'll have to do it."

Dane grimaced. "I'll go with you."

"No, stay here with Joy. Keep watch over her and Arden just in case someone shows up." Walker scrubbed his hands over his face as if he'd been awake far longer than the past twenty-four hours. "Angus is my piece-of-shit father. I've got to be the person to put an end to this, once and for all. He's fucked up too much in our lives already. Enough is enough."

"It's not your fault, you know." Dane kept his voice calm when Walker wanted to shout at the stars. "You can't control who you're born to and what decisions they make."

"That only makes it worse. I can't stop it. And yet I need to do everything I can to make sure he's not going to hurt Joy or you anymore. Either directly or because of the consequences of his dirty deeds."

"Not *everything*, though. Right?" Dane narrowed his eyes.

"If me rejoining Wildfire will get him to leave the three of you alone, to be a family, I'll do it." Walker gritted his teeth. If he donned the club colors and became VP under his father, it would be the end of the man Dane and Joy knew. They wouldn't want him back. He was afraid because he could so easily become exactly what his father had always wanted if he wasn't careful.

Without Dane and Joy, he'd lose touch with his positive emotions, all the things that made him a slightly decent human being. If he shut down that side of himself to survive, he had it in him to be ruthless. Just like his father.

He wouldn't stop at second in command. He'd take over. He'd make both Clive and Angus pay. It would be easy to embrace the hatred they inspired in him. He would succeed.

Walker would make his father pay for ruining his life.

And he would sacrifice every last shred of the man Dane and Joy cared about in the process. It would still be worth it, for them.

"You *are* my family, Walker." Dane's mouth twisted as if he'd bitten into a lemon. "If you don't get that by now, maybe you're right. Maybe I should focus on something —*someone*—else." He glanced over his shoulder.

"Go on." Walker jerked his chin toward their tiny home and the woman who'd already filled it to overflowing with life and love. It seemed warmer than it had since they'd built the thing, despite the freezing winter morning.

Dane shook his head. Still, he did as they both knew he would and went back to Joy…and Arden. After a few deep, calming breaths, Walker jogged down the stairs and across the lawn toward Hot Rides, where he could see lights on in the garage despite the early hour.

Since everyone who worked there lived in tiny homes —or a converted campervan in Ollie, Kyra, and Van's case —they'd taken to gathering in the shop's break room for meals and socializing. At least in the current weather conditions. During warmer months, they had an outdoor gathering area complete with picnic tables and a fire pit where they hung out together. With the Powertools crew in town, they'd drawn up plans to add a pavilion with an outdoor kitchen, some bench swings, and maybe even a pool down the road.

Though their individual living quarters were tight, it didn't feel constricting given the enormous workspace of the shop, the woods around them to explore, and their shared places. For Walker, the Hot Rides and Hot Rods compounds struck the perfect balance between privacy and the pack mentality he'd been used to first in Angus's motorcycle club and later in the military.

In every way, Hot Rides felt like home…but better.

Especially now that both Dane and Joy were here with him.

If there was even the smallest chance he could keep it that way, he had to try.

Walker marched into the garage, prepared to answer the questions written on everyone's faces when he stepped into the break room. He chuckled, then said, "I guess one benefit to a New Year's Eve without alcohol is no one's wrestling with a hangover this morning."

Gavyn grunted at that. "I told you guys you can drink if you want. Just because I can't...no, don't even want to anymore..."

Amber leaned in to kiss her husband's temple and smile. It had been a long, hard recovery for the man, but he was winning, day by day. If he could beat the odds, maybe Walker could defy his own circumstances. He'd never had that kind of positive role model before, though suddenly he seemed to be surrounded by them.

"Nah, we had plenty of fun without booze." Trevon reassured the Hot Rides garage owner. His wife, Devra, and their husband, Quinn, agreed.

"We sure did," added Devra, a petite Middle Eastern woman with a wicked grin. "Better to go home able to party in private rather than too drunk to do anything about all the energy we worked up dancing."

Wren turned to Devra and put her hand out for a high five. "That's what I'm talking about."

"No wonder you guys look nearly as beat as Walker," Gavyn teased before sobering up. "Did you sleep at all?"

"Nah." He shook his head before plopping into a seat beside Van. The beefy man sat next to his girlfriend Kyra and their boyfriend, Ollie. Across from them, Kason, Wren, and Jordan were huddled together too. It was enough to make him crazy given the fact that he'd left Dane and Joy behind in their cabin.

Joy Ride

If it could work for these guys...

There were so many reasons why he wasn't as lucky.

"Yeah, I figured the three of you might have spent the rest of the night like we did." Quinn wasn't grinning when he said it. "But if you had, you wouldn't look like trash this morning. What's up, Walker?"

Walker respected Quinn. Though Gavyn owned Hot Rides, Quinn—the shop manager—had really been the one to shape it into what it was becoming: a world-class operation with a knack for hiring the best in the business, even if they were quirky and unconventional. Although each of them would have been outcasts elsewhere, when they teamed up...anything seemed possible.

And there was never any judgment between them.

That didn't mean it was easy to lay all his business out for the world to see. Without some outlet, he'd fucking explode, so he closed his eyes and said, "One of us is a dad."

"And you don't know which of you it is?" asked Kason, the lead singer of the band Kyra played drums for.

Walker put his hands on his knees and squeezed, hard. "No."

"I'm sorry. That's rough." Kyra reached around Van and rubbed his back. Walker couldn't help it if he leaned a little closer to her reassuring touch. "I can tell you both care for her. I've never seen you react to someone like that before. In my mind, that's what really matters. So what's the problem?"

Care wasn't the word.

Walker loved Joy. Had from the moment her mother had moved in and he'd overheard Joy trying to convince the woman of what a colossal mistake she was making getting involved with Angus and the Wildfire outlaws.

He'd known right then she was smart and brave enough to speak the truth even when it wasn't going to go over well.

"To start, she's my stepsister." Walker was afraid to lift his gaze then.

"Were you raised together?" Ollie wondered.

"No. I mean, her mother married my father when I was almost seventeen. She's about a year and a half younger than me and Dane, who was my best friend, even back then." Walker swallowed hard.

Amber shot him a warning glance. "Before you decide to say whatever is about to come out of your mouth, you should consider the fact that all of the guys, and Sally, over at Hot Rods were in a similar situation. Tom adopted them in their late teens after they had rough starts. Since Sally, Alanso, and Eli are together—and all of the rest of them have a special bond, which involves a physical relationship on occasion—please be careful what you say next so I don't have to kick your ass or let one of them do it for me."

Walker blinked at her a few times. He hadn't really ever thought of it like that. Being around the Hot Rods family made it easy to see how perfect they were together. He'd never once questioned their bond or if what they were doing was right. It simply was, and they were each stronger for it.

What if he'd been screwing things up for nothing all this time?

"Let me guess." Wren jumped in then. The shop's welder was badass yet tender too. Especially when she was flanked by her two boyfriends, Jordan and Kason. "Dane had a monster hard-on for her back then, just like he does now. And you felt guilty about wanting your best friend's girl, especially because she was your stepsister."

Walker nodded. Was he that easy to read, or were they particularly good at understanding the intricacies and pitfalls of three-way relationships, given that they'd each managed to navigate one themselves?

"Well, now that you see you can have your cake and eat it too, so to speak," Ollie said, gesturing at himself, Van, and Kyra. "What's stopping the three of you—or should I say four—from becoming a unit?"

"My piece-of-shit father, mostly." Walker shifted his gaze to Jordan then. The man was an ex-special-agent for the government. He would understand the best. "He's the president of the Wildfire OMG. A motorcycle club, supposedly, though they do a lot more than ride bikes and shoot the shit, if you know what I mean. They're one-percenters and Joy's mom was my father's old lady, the main one anyway, until she was killed in a motorcycle accident when Dane and I were away in the military. After we finished our stint, we made the mistake of going back, because leaving Joy behind ate at us, and ended up fucking everything up worse instead."

"Hang on a second. I feel like you're speaking a foreign language." Devra tipped her head. "Can someone interpret for me?"

Quinn cleared his throat. "An OMG is an outlaw motorcycle gang and one-percenters are the most hardcore members of that lifestyle. It's not something to be taken lightly. These are people involved in organized crime, doing dirty work, and loving every minute of it. This is dangerous shit we're talking about."

Walker was glad both that Quinn understood the severity of the situation and also that he didn't have to rat on Wildfire himself. Even now the club rules ran deep in his blood. Outing his father and their brotherhood wasn't easy for him.

Fortunately, his silence in the face of Quinn's accusations was damning enough.

Jordan folded his hands over his stomach as if he wasn't as interested as Walker knew he was. "Is that why you left? You didn't want to be involved?"

"I couldn't do it." Walker sighed. "Over the years it seems like Angus has graduated from petty shit like intimidating people for kickbacks to selling illegal weapons and getting involved with drugs. Maybe even human trafficking. People die over this shit. That's not me, and it's sure as fuck not Dane. We risked our lives plenty of times in the service, saw our friends bleed out or get blown up in front of our eyes, but at least it was for something better than greed or ruining more lives—innocent or otherwise. Or we thought so at the time."

"Be honest. You left your old life to get Dane out, even though it meant leaving Joy behind." Quinn scratched his chin. "I can see how that had to be fucking wretched."

It sounded worse when Quinn said it out loud. Especially since Walker knew the guy had a thing about being abandoned. To Quinn, that was a cardinal sin. Walker would probably be lucky if the guy didn't toss him out on his sorry ass. "I didn't want to drag her into god knows what. Dane and I had nothing to offer her. Not compared to the way my dad's organization provides for her. Although he's a piece of shit, Angus is powerful, and he does keep her safe. Unlike Dane and I have ever been able to manage…"

Walker trailed off, remembering the sight of Dane

washing blood from her pale skin as she sobbed into his shoulder. Nothing had been the same after that.

"What happened?" Quinn asked.

"Clive, the club's sergeant-at-arms, staked a claim on Joy when she wasn't even legal yet. Raped her. Told everyone in the club she was his. It happened while we were out partying and being stupid. That night fucked everything up between her and Dane, who'd been dating on the down low. And me, who'd been perving on her, wishing I was Dane and...well, you know most of the rest. Everything imploded and we volunteered to go overseas. We've let her down so many fucking times..." Walker put his face in his hands and leaned his elbows on the table. The stakes were so much higher now that Joy was here, willing to walk away, *and* she had a child.

There could be no more mistakes.

Either by them entangling her in their affairs, or by deserting her when they shouldn't.

Every time he and Dane had shared a woman, Walker had imagined she was Joy. It was one reason he'd insisted they never sleep with the same woman more than once. It wasn't fair to act like he wanted a relationship with anyone other than the single person they couldn't have.

And as for Dane, Walker suspected the other guy went along with their arrangement because he didn't trust himself to take care of his partner. Not since Clive had attacked Joy, and shattered Dane's confidence along with his sense of self-worth.

They were a hot fucking mess. All of them.

"You have a chance to make it right now," Trevon said quietly.

"Maybe we would if it was only up to us, but there's more going on." Walker stood and began to pace. "My dear old dad is pissed that I don't want to follow in his footsteps. He has this twisted way of thinking, or maybe it's true in his world, about the importance of reputations. And by leaving…he feels I've taken away some of his clout. What does it say that his own son doesn't care to be part of his empire, you know? And now that Joy bailed too, it looks twice as bad. He's not going to stand for that kind of disrespect."

"Sounds like he needs to get over himself," Kason said.

"Maybe, but you guys need to be aware that if we stay, there's a chance shit could get ugly. I don't want to bring trouble to Hot Rides, or Middletown for that matter." Walker got to the point he'd been working up to. It hurt to admit it, but they had a right to know the truth and decide what to do about it up front.

"*You're* not doing anything except trying to live your life in peace," Quinn said. "If your father or people from his organization bring trouble, then we'll deal with them. The three of you and that precious baby better not be going anywhere or I'll be the one who takes offense. Not because I'll feel slighted or because of some petty ego-stroking bullshit. But because you belong here. With us."

Relief flooded Walker's veins, making his knees wobble as Quinn spoke his own feelings aloud. They truly were in sync. Thank God.

Gavyn was grinning at Quinn. "Sometimes you remind me so much of your brother, kid. Barracuda would be proud, you know. No, he *is* proud of the man you've become."

"Thanks," Quinn said with a hint of a boyish smile. "But seriously, we can take care of ourselves, and those around us. I hope you know that by now, Walker."

Kyra nodded at that. "After everything that happened

to me, I can promise I never felt as safe as when I was here. Hopefully Joy will come to know that security as well."

Van turned toward Walker and said, "Between me and Jordan, we can be proactive. We have plenty of staff and he has connections. We'll beef up security at the two shops until we see how things are going to play out. Sound good?"

"Yeah, absolutely." Walker breathed deep for the first time since Joy had walked through the garage door. If they stuck together, they just might be able to pull this off.

Van ran the security team for Kason Cox and the rest of his band. Jordan, given his background and his intimate relationship with the lead singer, had recently taken over personally guarding Kason's body while Van focused on protecting Kyra. Even Walker and Dane had lent a hand until her stalker had been apprehended.

Jordan leaned in. "Long term, exposing Wildfire and helping bring them down once and for all is going to be the best protection you can buy yourself. If you're willing to talk, I probably know some people who would like to listen to what you have to say about the workings of your father's operation. Set him up for some RICO stuff, you know? Your call. I know that could make things worse temporarily, but...it could be the way out for good."

Walker would have to think about that.

The long pause in their conversation started to turn awkward.

"Okay, so...what other excuses do you have? Let's hear them so we can tell you why you're being stupid." Wren laughed, drawing appreciative glances from Jordan and Kason. "Look, Jordan was pretty much the king of denial and I eventually cracked him. I can wear you down too."

"Hey—" Jordan acted offended though they all knew it was true.

Except Walker's objections weren't excuses if they were real issues. He didn't mind sharing another with his friends. Hopefully they could help him find a way around each of the things that had seemed insurmountable to him in the dead of night. This one might be trickiest of all.

"Joy's worried about making it on her own. She resents accepting help from us. She's stubborn as fuck." Walker clenched his teeth. In fact, the only person he knew that was more hardheaded than himself was Joy. If she put her foot down about taking handouts, he wouldn't be able to give her a damn thing. "Thing is, she's also super sheltered. In Wildfire she was essentially a trophy, and doesn't really have anything to fall back on when it comes to experience or getting a job."

"Well, I have a solution for that." Devra grinned. "I'll be looking for servers for the restaurant soon. I'd like to have our grand opening in about two months. If that's not too short of a maternity leave for her, she doesn't mind working hard for crappy pay, she thinks she can put up with a mouthy Yemeni woman as a boss, and doesn't mind eating a ton of food I'm going to beg her to taste-test because I'm paranoid and only want the best for the restaurant...she should consider herself hired."

"Seriously?" Walker stood, unable to contain his excitement. "You would do that on my word alone?"

"Hell yes." Devra smiled kind of sadly as she looked over at her husband, Trevon. "We know what it's like to face hard times. If Quinn hadn't taken a chance on us and hired Trevon, who knows where we'd be today? It would mean a lot to me if I could give someone else an opportunity to steer their life in the direction they'd like to go."

Walker didn't mean to crush her, but he wrapped Devra in a hug tight enough that she squeaked. He lifted her and swung her around, relieved and ecstatic that he could have at least that bit of good news to give Joy when he returned.

Except he didn't have to wait even that long. Because she was right there, behind him. He caught a glimpse of her as he twirled Devra.

Walker set his boss's wife down gently, before clearing his throat.

Behind him, someone only partially covered their laughter with a faux cough. But the flare of jealousy in Joy's eyes wasn't amusing to Walker. It was half-terrifying and half-arousing. Because if she didn't want anyone else touching him, maybe that meant she wanted to keep him for herself.

Dane hovered over her shoulder, Arden still snuggled in the crook of his arm. Was he ever going to put the baby down again? Walker could understand if he didn't.

Joy pasted on a smile that didn't reach her eyes. "I can come back later if I'm interrupting."

"No need." Devra smiled up at Joy. "Walker was just thanking me for offering you a job, even though it's really me who would thank you, if you'd accept it. I could desperately use some help."

"A job? Really? Doing what?" Joy flashed a wary glance at Walker, wondering what he'd gotten her into.

"I'm opening a restaurant and I need servers. It'll be ready to go in a couple months, but if you need more time with your baby, that's fine. We can make it happen." Devra inched closer, peering at the child Dane held with a wistful smile.

"I can start any time. Even sooner if you need help setting things up." Joy stepped forward as if *she* might pick Devra up and spin her around this time. "Are you sure? I've never even had a job before. I could totally suck."

Walker tried to school his dick not to perk up at that thought. Tried and failed. She sucked just fine.

"You'll do great." Devra beamed at her. "So is that a yes? Please?"

"Yes. God, yes." Joy did rush toward Devra then before wrapping her in a hug. "Thank you. You have no idea what this means to me."

"Actually, I do." Devra nodded slowly. It wasn't so long ago that she and Trevon had been living out of backpacks. "We're more alike than you might imagine. I know you didn't get to meet everyone last night so let me introduce you. This is my husband, Trevon."

She led Joy to the tall black man who was always quick to smile and had a knack for putting people at ease. After they'd shook hands, she then turned to Quinn, who could seem much more imposing given his dense tattoos, confidence, and solid build. "This is Quinn. My other husband."

Joy's eyes went wide. To her credit, she didn't show many other outward signs of her shock, but Walker and Dane knew her well enough to tell. She looked at him and he nodded.

Next Devra introduced her to Wren, Jordan, and Kason and then Kyra, Ollie, and Van.

When she'd made the circuit of the room Joy said, "So...you're all in committed threesomes?"

"Lucky us, huh?" Kyra said with a wiggle of her brows.

"Yeah," Joy said softly before glancing at Dane and then Walker. "Yeah, you are. Hell, I'd be happy if I could get a single guy to commit to me, never mind two studs like you ladies have. Fucking bitches, all of you."

The whole room exploded in laughter.

And just like that, Walker knew...Joy belonged there too.

8

Dane made another circuit of the living area floor, rocking and bouncing Arden. Her eyelids grew heavy and she drifted off in his arms. It had been a week since she'd come into his life, and he still never wanted to put her down. At least not until he looked at her serene face and imagined it twisted in pain, like Joy's had been that long ago night that Clive had possessed her against her will.

Then he knew that he could never survive failing Arden like he'd done to her mother.

So many times.

Even now, he wondered if he was doing it again. Living under the same roof with her and Walker was putting him in danger of losing his mind. Every shared look, laugh, and intimate moment that fooled him into thinking they could be more than roommates made him hungry for exactly that.

Yet none of them had acknowledged the carnal desire that still pulsed between them.

It didn't seem like the right time. Joy was a first-time

mother with a newborn and going through a total upheaval. Hell, he didn't even know if she was cleared to fool around after having Arden. There was so much he was clueless about. And every time they'd crossed that line in the past, it had led to disaster.

That didn't keep him from wanting her more with every passing second.

Dane didn't even have sex with Walker to help relieve some of the tension. Although he and his best friend had returned to sharing a bed, in order to give Joy and Arden the other room to themselves, Walker slept so near to the edge he had fallen off more than once. They didn't dare lie close lest they be tempted to put their hands on each other.

They wouldn't be able to keep from shouting the place down if they gave in to their passion now. Besides, it felt... wrong...to get it on and leave Joy out, with her so close and yet still impossible to reach.

Dane figured with the baby asleep and Joy also taking a well-deserved nap, he might have to sneak off to the bathroom for yet another jerkoff session. He was going to rub the damn thing raw if he wasn't careful.

His frustration wasn't only physical, though that was the simplest form to cure.

Joy had been up with a fussy Arden all night. And when he'd offered to take over minding the baby for a while, she'd shut him out, which was probably justified. Sure, she'd said it was out of respect for his work schedule the next day. But Dane knew the truth.

She didn't trust him and Walker. And why should she?

Not even Joy could go without rest forever, though. And when she'd finally succumbed after he'd finished his shift, he'd promised to take Arden to the shop, where

Amber was hanging out with Gavyn now that she was officially on leave to prepare for their own impending new addition. They could provide backup if he needed it. Surprisingly, so far he hadn't.

Dane thought he'd even managed to get Arden's diaper on right, though she'd peed on him in the process. He debated handing her off to Amber now, while she slept, so that he could make some progress on his special project. In fact, if Walker had kept going on it after he'd gone home to check on their girls, he might have finished it by now.

They'd been working on a portfolio piece for the shop, something to demo their metal fabrication skills for prospective customers. And when Joy arrived, both he and Walker had known what to do with the motorcycle. It screamed her name.

The bike was a highly modified café racer from the seventies with a lot of retro flair. It was white with white rims and Mustang Sally had taken it to her paint shop at Hot Rods to add pink details that made it both feminine and sassy simultaneously. It was petite and lightweight, easy for a woman of Joy's stature to handle. Everyone in the shop had contributed to the project, Wren especially, but Quinn and Trevon too. Hell, even Gavyn had pitched in.

Now they only had to hope she still enjoyed riding. He'd understand if her mother's death or all the years in between when he'd taught her to drive a motorcycle and now had erased her love of the wind in her hair.

If so, he prayed she would understand what they were trying to give her—the freedom she so desperately craved.

Dane strolled into the garage in time to see Walker arranging and rearranging the ribbons of a giant white bow. Walker never gave a shit about stuff like that, but it seemed he wanted their gift to be absolutely flawless, too. Dane smiled. Maybe there was hope for them yet.

He looked up and grinned before swiping an imaginary piece of dust from the gleaming fuel tank. "Hey. How's it look?"

"Pretty damn fine, if I do say so myself." Dane admired their work and the proof of what they could accomplish together.

"Maybe we should go get Joy," Walker suggested.

Dane shook his head. "Let her sleep. There will be plenty of time later."

"For what?" Joy asked, making them both spin around guiltily. "Is Arden okay? Sorry, I woke up when I couldn't hear her anymore. I think it's some kind of weird instinct."

Dane could detect the panic underlying her admission. Apparently so could everyone else.

"She's absolutely wonderful," Amber called from where she was rocking Arden in the swing they'd set up for her in the office. "Don't you worry about that."

"Then..." Joy started to say before she noticed Dane and Walker standing proudly next to their work. She canted her head, then asked, "What's this?"

"It's for you," Walker said simply. "I know how much it means to you to be independent. You've already got a car, but everyone knows a motorcycle is different. Besides, it's what we know, what we're good at, and what we have to share with you. I hope you like it."

"A motorcycle? For me?" Joy's eyes widened. Then they turned glassy.

Shit, was she going to cry? Joy never cried.

"You hate it?" Dane's stomach cramped. "I told Walker

you might not want one after what happened to your mom…"

"No. It's…perfect." She smiled, something he'd only seen when she was playing with Arden lately. "You know Mom and Angus would never let me have my own. Those times when you guys would take me somewhere our parents couldn't see and let me ride were some of my favorites. I felt so…liberated."

Dane nodded. "We want you to know that you're free now. Even if you're staying with us for the moment. You're your own person and make your own decisions these days. We never intend to take that away from you."

Joy's breathing hitched.

"No one has ever done something this thoughtful for me before." She sniffled. "I can really just go. Whenever I want?"

Dane tried not to panic at that thought. He had to mean what he said. Keeping Joy like a caged bird wasn't what any of them wanted. Look where that had gotten them so far.

"Of course." Walker leaned in then, taking her hand and toying with her fingers. "We would never try to own you, Joy. If you choose to stay here, with us, Dane and I will be happy. We're certainly not kicking you out. But it's always up to you. You can do anything, be anything. We'll help you get wherever you need to go. I hope you realize that, at least."

Joy hesitated, then nodded. "Thank you. In that case, will you watch Arden a little longer so I can take this out for a test drive?"

"Take all day if you like." Amber stared dreamily at Arden as she sang softly to the still-sleeping baby.

Trevon, Quinn, and Wren followed the three of them

as Joy walked the bike out of the shop and a little way down the driveway to, hopefully, avoid waking Arden. She climbed on and started the bike like a pro.

From the sidelines, Trevon whistled. "There's nothing sexier than a woman who knows how to ride."

"It's been a while." Joy bit her lip as she zipped up her leather jacket and picked up the helmet they'd bought for her. "What if I'm too rusty?"

Quinn grinned at her, some of his mischievous side peeking out. "It's one of those things you never forget, like swimming or fucking."

Instead of being embarrassed or horrified, Joy laughed. Dane could have hugged the guy. They were watching Joy blossom right in front of them. For the first time, he realized how much more beautiful she was when she felt confident and secure in her place. Stunning. So damn attractive his dick ached.

Nothing could have shocked Dane more than when she turned to him, beaming, and asked, "Want to come with me?"

"Hell yes," he answered before he could think better of it.

Walker glared at him, probably equal parts jealous and wary that Dane would fuck up their plan. But she'd asked and he'd answered honestly. In the past, he'd tried to control the situation or let Walker do it, and where had that gotten them?

Nowhere. From then on, he was simply going to live in the moment and see what happened.

"Well, hop on then." Joy held the bike and scooted forward just a bit to make room for him.

"Don't hate me. I'm weak," he muttered to Walker.

"Fuck you," Walker grumbled as Dane crossed to Joy's bike and threw his leg over it.

He wrapped his arms around her waist, not because his balance required the hold but because it was the perfect excuse to do what he'd wanted to for seven excruciatingly long days now.

Nah, more like years.

Dane pulled her close to his chest and squeezed her before letting her settle into place as she checked the dials and tested the brakes.

"Ready?" she asked, her voice slightly raspier than usual.

"So ready," he said.

She grinned, then revved the engine before putting it into gear and taking off as smoothly as if she'd done it the day before instead of in ancient history.

Joy was cautious, yet sure of herself and her abilities. She trusted the machine they'd chosen and tailored especially for her. If nothing else, Dane was positive he and Walker were good at what they did. They'd never have hacked it at Hot Rides otherwise, and working in the shop had honed their talents even further.

"Hang on," she cautioned him, so he did, imagining he might never let her go again.

9

Dane's fingers stroked Joy's soft leather-covered belly and imagined what he might do if there were far fewer layers of clothes between them. He adored the changes her body had gone through since they were essentially still kids, no matter how grown they'd thought they were. She was lush—all woman. And when she punched it and gave the motorcycle more power, he whooped as they shot forward.

Being with her was exhilarating. These had always been the best moments of his life. Especially when Walker was with them too. Maybe they should have let her drive from the beginning—where might she have taken them if only they'd given her the chance?

Dane swore then and there that he would do better this time.

He wished he wasn't wearing a helmet so he could bury his face in the crook of her neck and kiss the soft skin there while they flew along the country roads. Of course, that would probably be a terrible idea. His cock didn't seem to care. It hardened, pressing up against the swells of Joy's ass. Despite the denim of their jeans, she had to feel how much she excited him.

They rode together, leaning and swaying as they took turn after turn.

Between the rumble of the engine, holding Joy in his arms, and the way her body cradled his cock, Dane was a little concerned he might embarrass himself. So he squeezed his knees around her until she glanced over her shoulder.

"Pull over?" he shouted.

She found the next appropriate spot and did just that, guiding them to the shoulder and bracing her foot on the ground like a seasoned veteran, which did nothing to make him want her any less.

"Everything okay?" she asked as she rotated to face him.

"Yeah. I mean, I think so." Dane climbed off the bike and strode a few feet into the woods. Sticks and leaves crackled beneath his boots. At least it had warmed up some from the cold snap they'd had recently. He braced himself on a pine tree and tried to get his head on straight. It was hard to do when he was high on adrenaline and Joy.

"You have to pee or something?" she called. "Go ahead, I'm not looking."

Dane snorted at that. After everything they'd been through—hell, they might even have created a child together—he wouldn't be in the least bit concerned about whipping it out in front of her. Especially not with his back turned. He spun to face her. "No, sorry. I just needed a second."

"Please tell me you're freaking out because you're as turned on as I am right now," Joy rasped, as she shook out her hair and set her helmet aside. She was his every fantasy come to life.

A grown-up version of the kid he'd crushed on, completely capable of caring not only for herself, but another human being. She was glorious and he wanted her like he'd never lusted after any woman before or since.

Dane beckoned her, curling his fingers toward his palm. She came, as if drawn by the elements, the same ones that hadn't let him escape her pull for very long throughout his life. No matter how far he ran, he would never be impervious to her allure. He was sure of that now.

"You know I am." He glanced down at where his hard-on distorted his pants, the hem of his leather jacket just a bit too short to obscure the evidence of it.

"I was hoping you hadn't stuck a gun in your pocket or something." She winced. "I never can tell with you…or Walker."

"I don't carry anymore." He frowned. "Though maybe I should start again…"

Joy shook her head. She stepped closer and put two fingers over his mouth, making him long to draw them inside and suck on them until she let him do far more interesting things to her. "I'm happy to be away from that lifestyle. I only meant that you never need me as badly as I need you."

"What?" Dane stared at her, absolutely dumbfounded.

There was no way he was going to let her live with that lie another moment.

Dane whispered, "I hope this isn't the wrong thing to do. I'm not sure anymore with you, Joy. But I have to taste you. To show you just how much I've missed you, now and always."

"Do it," she urged, her eyes pleading even as she demanded he follow through.

He cupped her cheeks in his palms and drew her face to him while he leaned in to bridge the gap between their mouths. The first brush of his lips against hers sent a lightning bolt of desire straight to his balls. They clenched and made him shudder.

"Fuck," he muttered into her mouth. "I could come just from tasting you, I swear."

Joy whimpered as if the admission of his desire was enough to wring a similar response from her. He stayed still, giving her time to adjust to their reconnection, but she didn't seem to approve of his hesitation. She fisted the back of his jacket in her hands and crushed them together from pelvis to shoulders before feeding him her sweet moans and the tip of her tongue.

He let her take whatever she wanted from him.

If he were Walker, he would have assumed control, guided the exchange, but... That wasn't Dane, not anymore and probably not ever. Truth was, he'd always felt Joy would wake up one day and realize she was far too strong-willed for him. Instead, she seemed to relish the reins he gave her. She thrived, transforming into a wildcat.

Joy switched her hold. She wrapped her arms around his neck and backed him into the tree. His shoulders hit the bark hard enough to make him grunt. Then she started to climb him, or at least it seemed like she might. Her leg was hooked at his hip. So he grabbed it, holding it there as Joy hopped.

And that's how he found himself holding her with her

legs spread around him. They ground together as their tongues met and swirled around each other. His hands shifted so that he cupped her lush bottom and squeezed, thinking how much Walker would love to feel her like this.

He'd always been the ass man of the two of them.

Aside from her eyes, Dane had a thing for her breasts, which were fuller than he remembered and also mashed against him as they made out with abandon.

Joy kneaded his shoulders. He was certain that if they'd been naked she would have sank her sharp little nails into the flesh there, driving him to stop thinking and simply react the way his body—and heart—always did to her.

She undulated against him, simulating the sex they'd had that night he'd never forget. The one where she'd rocked his world and ruined both him and Walker for threesomes with anyone else. It had been a record dry spell for them. At least with other people. They'd remained exclusive to each other, realizing no one else could make them feel the way this woman had when she'd bared herself to them and let them have all of her.

Her generosity meant even more to him now that he knew they'd been her first lovers.

If Dane had his way, it would be Walker instead of the tree behind him.

He spun around, leaning Joy up against the imposing pine and pinning her body between it and him. The moan that echoed through the forest made Dane sure that Joy remembered just as clearly as he did what it had been like when she'd been trapped between him and his best friend. Walker hadn't taken it easy on her, or on Dane, commanding that they perform for him and refusing to stop fucking them both until he'd smashed every last illusion of civility between them.

Dane kissed Joy now like he had then. Like he'd always wanted to when they'd been too young to know how to do it right. They'd both grown and gotten so much better at it. He used every ounce of finesse he had to bring her pleasure, and it seemed to work.

Joy cried out his name, took a sharp breath, then went back for more.

She devoured him.

Pouring herself into the exchange, she granted him as much ecstasy as she took.

Dane was so absorbed in Joy and the way she made him feel, as if he was still racing over the pavement even though they were standing still, he lost track of their surroundings. In the back of his mind, he might have heard something, but he ignored it in favor of continuing to drown in the pleasure Joy brought him.

Until it grew loud enough that he had to give the racket his full attention.

And that's when he realized that someone was coming straight for them, charging through the brush. They weren't even trying to be subtle about it.

He blinked, trying to get his bearings. They didn't have enough time to make it to Joy's bike. Whoever it was would be on them before they could reach the shiny café racer and start the engine.

An image of Joy, shot in the back and crashing to the cold forest floor, sent chills down his spine.

Instincts took over. He grabbed Joy and shoved her behind him, spinning so that she was blocked from whoever was approaching rapidly by his body and the giant tree they'd been making out under.

Fuck! How could he have been so reckless?

Dane braced himself, balling his fists, raising them and spreading his legs. It wasn't much but he was trained in hand-to-hand combat, both by his experiences hanging around Wildfire and the military drills that had honed his natural capabilities.

Except it would be pretty dumb to punch a deer. Especially the enormous buck that launched itself over the trunk of a fallen pine and kept sprinting right past them, chased by who knew what.

Behind him, Joy chuckled. "Wait until I tell Walker you were ready to fight a buck."

Dane wasn't laughing. He wished he could pummel himself instead. When the hell was he going to learn how to take care of Joy properly? What if it had been Arden he'd put at risk?

"We should head back," Dane mumbled, already marching off toward the motorcycle they'd left in plain view on the side of the road.

How had he allowed himself to be so irresponsible with Joy's safety? Anyone could have come across them there out in the open, while he made them vulnerable—both to attack and to another colossal fuck up that would tear them apart. This time for good.

He'd only proven, once again, that he was worthless when it came to looking out for Joy and what was in her best interests.

"Dane..." She reached for him, but let her fingers drop when she realized he'd already mentally retreated. Same as always.

They were doomed to repeat the same cycle over and over. Only he wasn't certain his heart could take it anymore. "Let's go. We've been gone too long already. Walker will be worried."

"About you, not me." Joy deflated. Every last sparkle of mischief that had twinkled in her eyes while they kissed had been snuffed by his stupidity. "You're right. I should check on Arden."

Without another word, they got on her bike. She checked both ways carefully before pulling onto the road. Joy stayed just under the speed limit, perfectly cautious and controlled, as they wound their way back to Hot Rides.

Unlike he had on the way to the woods, Dane made sure to keep a buffer of space between him and Joy so she couldn't tell that even after all that chaos, his body still wished things could be different.

Too bad his brain knew better.

10

"Hey, Joy. You ready for round two?" Devra asked her as she waved a pie cutter over the sweet honey cake she'd whipped up for their girls-only retreat. Bint al-Sahn. Joy had learned the name of it, repeating it until she'd pronounced it precisely like Devra since it would be on the menu of her restaurant. She was going to sell a million pieces.

Devra had kicked her two husbands out so that she could give Joy a sneak peek of the items she'd be serving. Kyra, Wren, and Amber had joined in because...well, baked goods and gossip. Why not?

It felt odd to have friends, people who weren't sucking up to her because of who her stepfather was or trying to use her to get to him in some sick and twisted way. It had been a while since she'd allowed herself to make those sorts of personal connections because it had always turned sour and sometimes downright dangerous.

With Devra, Wren, Kyra, and Amber—and the rest of the Hot Rods and Powertools ladies she'd met since arriving in Middletown, there were a ton of them to get to know—she didn't have to worry about what they were scheming...unless it was some ill-disguised matchmaking plot.

"Yeah." Joy figured she didn't need to worry about recovering her waistline as soon as possible post-baby since Walker and Dane didn't seem interested in rekindling their relationship. Dane had practically ignored her since their disastrous liaison. They were driving her to cake. "Hit me. I could use another slice."

Wren and Kyra exchanged glances at that, as if Joy had kicked the door wide open, inviting their curiosity. They might as well air out all her dirty laundry. It was getting awkward to know these women so well, spend so much time in their company, and yet keep so much to herself. It felt like she was lying by omission about some vital pieces of herself.

"So, totally to be nosy...how *are* things going with Dane and Walker?" Devra plopped down next to Joy, handed her a plate of flaky dessert, and met her gaze so she couldn't evade the conversation. Not that she cared to, really. It was a relief to have someone to talk to about the situation.

Women who could understand and wouldn't automatically think she was nuts for lusting after both of her housemates or wanting them at all, given their history. She'd never had a sounding board like that before. Maybe with their advice and experience in her corner, things could go differently between her and the guys this time.

God knew they weren't figuring it out on their own, even after repeated attempts.

"Um, it's okay. I guess?" Joy winced. "We haven't killed each other yet and they haven't evicted me."

"Girl, I think your bar is a little low." Wren snickered.

"Probably. But in my experience, it's better not to set yourself up for inevitable disappointment." Joy shoveled a huge chunk of cake into her mouth. Damn, it was good. Devra's restaurant was going to be a hit. She hoped that meant she'd make decent tips.

"I'm sorry you've been let down so often." Devra frowned.

"You know what's exceeding my expectations? Your baking." Joy focused on her plate and forked up another bite.

"You're not wrong, but flattery won't get them to leave you alone." Amber shot the other ladies a pointed glare. "They're like leeches once they latch on. They're going to suck the juicy details out of you, so you might as well come clean and save them the effort."

Joy laughed, choking on her mouthful. Once she'd swallowed it, humming in delight, she confessed, "I mean, in some ways it's great, living with Dane and Walker again. It feels just like it did when we shared Angus's house. Except better because there isn't Wildfire shit hanging over our heads all the time, making us paranoid. Plus, they've taken to Arden like…well, like she's their own."

"That doesn't surprise me as much as it seems to shock you." Kyra smiled softly. "Walker and Dane are good guys. They'll do the right thing. Besides, how could they resist Arden…or you?"

"I don't know about all that." Joy waved off the second part of Kyra's declaration.

"They must have seriously fucked up with you to make you doubt what is obvious to everyone else—you know, the fact that they drool over you." Wren shook her head. "Dumbasses. What did they do?"

"They have a habit of leaving me. I don't want to get

too attached. It would hurt so bad if they turned their backs on me again. Worse if they did it to their daughter. I would never forgive them for that." There, she'd said it.

"I don't know why they haven't stuck around in the past," Devra said. "But when they look at you, they change. They have a soft spot when it comes to you. If they didn't care, they wouldn't have invited you into their home. They're doing well enough they could have set you up somewhere on your own but they want you close. They love you."

"Sometimes that's not enough, is it?"

"Worse, sometimes I think it can make things more complicated." Wren sighed. "Jordan left me for ten years after our first partner was killed in the line of duty."

"Oh my God." Joy set down her somehow empty plate and fork on the coffee table with a clatter. "I'm so sorry. How did you get him back?"

"It's a long story. I'll tell you some other time, when we're not talking about you. Suffice it to say that it wasn't easy for any of us. But if Walker and Dane are the guys for you, you're going to have to fight for them." Wren leaned in. "It will be worth it."

"Will it, though? Or am I foolish for hoping things could work out after so many failures? The stakes are so much higher this time. I won't be able to handle it." Joy looked at the exposed rafters of the tiny home Devra shared with Trevon and Quinn, hoping the other women couldn't tell how close to bawling she was.

"Oh, honey, none of us has had it easy. Hell, Kyra and Ollie almost died after one of their arguments with Van recently." Amber gestured at the perky blonde. Joy hated to admit it, but she'd felt a little bitter about the women and their perfect lives and their perfect men.

Had she had it wrong?

Maybe she needed to be more persistent. If she gave up, then she was doomed to a life without the two men she dreamed of. She couldn't quite believe it could be possible. "Really?"

"Yeah." Devra put her hand on Joy's knee and squeezed. "Trust me. We've been where you are, in one way or another. Even Amber and Gavyn broke up once before he got treatment for his addiction and they figured things out for good. *Perfect* relationships come with plenty of potholes to swerve around."

If things had worked out for these women, why should it be different for her?

"Just promise us you'll think about what would really make you happy," Kyra said. "And if that's those two gearheads, then we're all in to help you scheme up some ways to get back together with them. Fair warning, it might involve rope, sexy lingerie, and some inventive positions." She rubbed her hands together.

Amber stood, somewhat unsteadily and shoved Kyra from the arm of the couch onto the cushion as she made her way to the bathroom. That did nothing to erase the evil grin from her face.

"I guess what bothers me the most is that I've been trying so hard to break free and now that I kind of am, at least for the moment, all I want is to be theirs. Is that dumb?" Joy bared her soul. Why stop short at this point?

"Absolutely not." Wren was serious when she said, "Independence is great, but partnering with people you choose is even better. Going through life solo is hard."

"And lonely," Joy added.

"That too." Devra nodded.

Joy picked up her plate and carried it to the kitchen

along one wall of the intimate space. She needed a moment to breathe and to think. Because what they were saying was ringing true. Maybe her lingering feelings for Dane and Walker made her loyal and not stupid.

Maybe they deserved one more chance...if she could convince them to take it.

She thought about Dane and how frantically he'd kissed her, but also about how he'd stormed off afterward. "I just might need that rope after all."

"Woohoo!" Kyra bounced on the couch and pumped her fist.

Until something interrupted their rowdy encouragement.

"Guys?" Amber called from the bathroom. The hint of panic in her tone had them on their feet in an instant, Joy at the front of the pack.

She raced to the door and said, "You okay?"

"I think so but...my water broke." Amber sounded shaky. "This feels really...real."

"You're okay. Wash your hands and come on out. Where's your bag for the hospital?" Joy asked, preparing to run over to the house for her.

"It's in the garage office." After the running water cut off and a paper towel crumpled, Amber opened the door. Her chest rose and fell in rapid, shallow drops that Joy could relate to. She'd felt the same trepidation when she'd realized Arden was on the way.

"Okay, I'm going to grab it. Will someone else call Gavyn?" Joy took a few steps toward the door.

"No. Damn it!" Amber latched onto Joy's sleeve and yanked. "My sister had a big meeting this afternoon. They're talking to an automotive chain about doing a nationwide deal for Hot Rods branded components. She's supposed to be my coach. Gavyn is there too in case there's opportunity for Hot Rides to get in on the action. It's super important. I don't want to interrupt them before they close the deal. Shit!"

"Don't worry. You've probably got plenty of time before active labor starts." Joy recalled how terrified she'd been when her water had broken in the middle of the night. With no one else to rely on, she'd gotten in her car and zoomed toward Dane's cabin, calling the midwife to meet her on the way.

She blinked the memories aside. Without some idea of what to expect, the first time experiencing childbirth could be terrifying along with excruciatingly painful.

Amber clutched Joy's hand hard enough to risk cracking a few bones. "Is this a good time to mention I've sort of been having contractions for a while? I was thinking they weren't serious but…maybe…"

"Don't worry. You're going to be fine. Do you remember your breathing exercises? Stay calm and relaxed and things will go more smoothly. This is more of a marathon than a sprint." Joy kept her voice even and low although she simultaneously led Amber to their jackets where Devra helped her get dressed so Joy could do the same for herself.

They were going to the hospital. Pronto.

"You know what, I've got the bag." Wren jogged for the door. "I saw it in the office. I'll grab it and meet you out front."

Kyra seemed a little shell shocked, and looked to Joy. So did Devra. Having these women defer to her did a lot for her battered ego. She might not know how to weld, or be a drummer in a famous band, or own her own business, but she had brought a new life into the world, pretty much on her own.

"Will you stay with me?" Amber peered at Joy with wide, worried eyes. "At least until Gavyn and Nola get to the hospital? Please?"

The sentiment hit her straight in the chest. No one had ever needed her like that before. She'd always felt useless or unwanted. From the time her mother had shacked up with Angus, to watching Dane and Walker leave for the military, and definitely the morning after they'd made love and she'd woken up to a cold, empty bed, there'd always been something missing. This feeling right here. "Of course I will. I'll stay as long as you'd like."

"Thank you," Amber threw her arms around Joy, squashing her in a bear hug.

"It's truly my pleasure." Joy wondered if *this* was what she was meant to do.

After all, now that she had the opportunity to do anything she chose with the rest of her life, it was time to start making some decisions about what exactly it was she intended to pursue. Maybe she'd reach out to her own midwife in the coming days and see what steps she'd need to take to become official. If she could help women through some of the most excruciating, exhilarating, and profound moments of their lives, what better calling could there be?

She held Amber's hand until she loaded the woman in the passenger seat of her car. Kyra, Devra, and Wren piled in the backseat. Devra said, "I texted Quinn and asked him to let Gavyn and Nola know what's up the moment the meeting is finished. Amber's mom and Tom are going to meet us at the hospital. Want me to text Walker and

Dane so they know they're on Arden duty for the rest of the day?"

"Would you, please?" Joy wondered what it said that she didn't even hesitate leaving her baby home, unsupervised for an extended period, with Dane and Walker. Okay, fine, she knew what it said.

She still loved and trusted them, despite everything that had come before.

And soon she would have to do something about that.

11

Walker poked his head into Amber's hospital room, not surprised in the least to see Joy leaning up against the far wall with a satisfied smile as she watched the rest of the Hot Rides fawn over Amber and Gavyn's brand-new son.

He remembered that look on her face. It was similar to the one she'd had after he and Dane had fucked her senseless. It made his cock stand up and take notice.

Not now.

"Come on, Walker. Meet Noah." Gavyn waved him in, making him a little unsure about his place. He was still one of the new people around the shop and had hardly settled in before Joy had appeared. To be included in a moment as pivotal as this in their lives...it meant something to him. Something he hoped he had earned.

He glanced at Joy, who nodded encouragingly, before inching closer. The infant was swaddled in a blanket that turned it into a baby burrito. Even so, it was terrifyingly small. Breakable. So much responsibility it made him rear up and blurt, "He's so tiny. Even Arden is way bigger than this."

The women laughed and Eli—the owner of Hot Rods—shook his head. "Hey, man, it's not all about size."

Bryce, the tallest and broadest of the entire Hot Rods gang, rumbled, "Oh yes, it is."

From the other side of the room, Joy snorted. "You know, Arden was even smaller than Noah when she was born. She weighed ten ounces less and was three inches shorter."

"No. Seriously?" Walker couldn't imagine that. She was delicate enough as it was.

"Yep." Joy looked to Amber and said, "Enjoy every minute. They go by so fast."

The other woman beamed, unable to take her eyes off her husband and their baby. "I will. Thank you again for staying with me and keeping me calm when I would have totally lost it. You were a huge help."

Walker's chest puffed up at that. It made him proud that his friends saw how decent Joy was. In fact, he couldn't ever remember someone appreciating her for her accomplishments instead of who she belonged to before. He hoped this was the first of many times he'd get to see that.

"You should go and get some rest," Amber told Joy. "You were up with me the entire seventeen hours of pure torture Noah put me through and every moment since. Don't worry, baby. Mommy loves you anyway," she cooed at her son.

In that instant, Walker wondered who'd been there for Joy. Had she gotten through Arden's delivery by herself? Holy shit. She was even stronger than he'd realized. And

Joy Ride

they were even more terrible for having left her to do it alone.

Superwomen like Joy needed to sleep too. He realized then that she was bracing herself on the wall, not hanging back to avoid intruding.

"Congratulations, guys." He slapped Gavyn on the back and nodded at Amber. "But yeah, I'm taking Joy home."

"I drove here. I can get myself back to Hot Rides." Joy's stubborn statement would have held more weight if she hadn't swayed on her feet as she shoved off the wall.

"Like hell." He crossed to her and put his arm around her waist, drawing her to his side. "Give me your keys. One of the Hot Rods guys can bring my bike back later...right?"

He didn't even bother to look over his shoulder as Alanso volunteered to do it.

"See? Now, let's go."

Joy groused but relented. "Fine. But only because I'm too pooped to argue with you."

"Perfect." He led her toward the door as they said their goodbyes.

Walker tried not to focus on Joy's lush curves where they pressed into him, but it would have been impossible to ignore how perfectly she fit with him. He kept reminding himself, until they reached the ground floor and he walked her out to her car, that he'd probably get arrested if he trapped her up against the elevator wall and had his way with her.

"Where's Arden? How is she?" Joy wondered. "I've never been away from her for so long."

She really was fatigued if it took her until then to ask. "She's great. Having a blast with the other kids at Hot

Rods. Dane is there and Nova is showing him the dad-ropes. If it's okay with you, I think we should let them hang out there for the day so you can catch up on your sleep."

"Wow. Even though I miss her so much, that sounds like one hell of an indulgence." Joy scrubbed her face with her hands. "But I can't. She's probably running out of milk by now."

"Dane has the emergency formula you told him about, but if you pumped at the hospital I can run supplies over there after you're tucked in." He didn't think anything of it.

To Joy though... She chuckled, shaking her head. "I can't believe this is my life right now. It's so different from just a month ago."

"How so?"

"I'm not alone. There are people around I can rely on and who will help out so I don't have to take care of everything myself. And I haven't looked over my shoulder in probably longer than is wise." She frowned. "They are being careful with her there, right? They know about Wildfire?"

"Angus himself would have a hard time making it past the guys at the garage." Walker squeezed her. "They're taking shifts coming over to the hospital. I promise, Arden is safe with them."

"Okay." She relaxed, letting her head loll against his shoulder as they approached her car. How did she still have faith in him and his word after all this time?

Probably it was only because she was somewhere between barely awake and passed out. Bleary and punch drunk. Also probably why she started rambling. "If you think I'm tired now, you should have seen me in the first few weeks after Arden was born. I cried every day. I had no idea what I was doing or if she would be okay stuck with me and only me. I was a mess."

Walker opened the passenger door and tucked her inside, fastening her seatbelt for her when she sat there, her arms limp at her sides. "You did so good, Joy. With Arden, coming to find us, and supporting Amber yesterday and today. I've always been impressed by how you take care of everyone around you, even though others haven't always done the same for you."

"I guess I know how shitty it feels and I don't ever care to let someone else be that disappointed if I can help it." Her eyes were already closed, so she didn't see how her unintentional barbs slashed him to the core.

Walker couldn't say what made him do it—stupidity, most likely—but leaning over her, smelling her baby powder scent, and being reminded of the wounds he'd inflicted on her, he couldn't help but kiss her temple before he retreated and shut the door, maybe harder than he should have.

He rounded her car and stood there for a few seconds, bracing his palms against the frame above the window while he got himself under control. By the time he slid behind the wheel, her head had tipped forward. He wouldn't be surprised if she dozed off before they'd even left the parking lot.

When he started the engine, she jerked, her hand flying out to grab the door and splay across the console simultaneously. "What's that? Who's there?"

"Hey, it's me," Walker murmured. "We're going home now. To Hot Rides. Where you can get some proper rest."

After her wide-eyed stare pinged wildly around the interior of the car, she slumped against the seat once more. "I've been on edge. Was so afraid Angus was going to find us or try to take Arden from me."

"I know. And I'm sorry. I wish you'd got in touch with us sooner." He cursed himself silently for bailing on her, even if they hadn't known she was pregnant. They'd taken precautions but apparently that didn't always matter.

"How the hell was I supposed to do that?" She shot him a glare. "Fuck, I wouldn't even have known where to find you if it hadn't been for Clive accidentally giving me a clue."

"At least he's finally been good for something, that fucker." Walker gnashed his teeth as he always did when he thought of Angus's chief thug.

"Don't tell Dane." Joy blew out a mirthless laugh.

"Wouldn't dare. He has every right to hate Clive. So do you. I wouldn't take that from either of you." Walker understood exactly how much Dane had suffered because of the other man. Both indirectly because of what he'd done to Joy and more profoundly because of what that one night had cost them both.

"I won't forgive him—ever—for what he did to me. But over time I came to understand that in his own warped way, he really did think he was protecting me." Joy's face crumpled, and for a moment Walker was terrified she was going to bawl. Because then he really would have to hunt the bastard down and kill him. "I think in the end, he hurt Dane worse than me. He's not the same as he used to be, is he?"

"Lately he seems more like the guy I knew." Walker could be honest about that at least. "You're good for him, Joy. Always have been. And Arden, well, she's good for everyone."

"You included?" Of course she would ask.

"Of course." Even if he was scared shitless about how much he loved having the baby around.

"Then why don't you hold her?" Joy wondered, suddenly seeming more alert.

He wished she'd go back to sleep so they didn't have to discuss difficult topics. "I do."

"Not really. You pick her up if she's crying or when it's time to feed her if Dane isn't around to do it for you. But as soon as you're not obligated, you put her down. Does it bother you that she could be Dane's?" Joy stared out the window when she asked, as if the answer might be more than she could bear.

"Look at me."

She didn't.

"Joy..."

Slowly, she turned her head.

"I already love Arden so much it terrifies me. What if she's not mine? What if you and Dane take off with her and leave me behind this time?"

She stammered, "I wouldn't. *We* would never."

"Why not? That's exactly what you should do." Walker's heart pounded in his chest so hard he thought he could hear it over the purr of the car's engine as he merged onto the highway. "Without ties to me, Angus will probably leave you alone. You can live together, in peace, and forget about all the bullshit Wildfire put you through. You can heal and grow. As a family."

"You *are* Dane's family." Joy shot him a look that clearly said she thought he was stupid.

"I'm his crutch." Walker shook his head. He wished Dane was there with them right now. They'd been needing to hash this out for a while. It was time for him to cut the other man loose so Walker could stop holding him back. Especially now that Joy and happily ever after was within reach again.

"What do you mean by that?" Joy narrowed her eyes. "My brain isn't functioning at full capacity. Spell it out."

"When his whole world caved in, after you two split apart, he leaned on me. Because of our relationship, and how we stuck together, he never had to face it and grieve fully. Never had to address the things that are broken deep inside him. And now, he should already be healed and ready to take on this new adventure with you. Instead, he's still damaged." Walker had fucked up again. "It's my fault. I just...I was selfish. I didn't want to let that part of my past go because I knew if he went on without me, I would be lost."

For a moment there was dead silence in the car. The yellow line whizzing by was all he had to anchor him as he waited for Joy to say something. Anything.

"Wow, Walker. I don't think I've ever heard you be so... honest. And sincere." Joy put her hand on his knee and squeezed. That did not have any sort of reassuring effect on him. Instead, it riled him up. He considered swerving onto the side of the road to do something unwise about it. Too bad the backseat of her car was far too small for what he had in mind.

Oh, yeah. It was also the dumbest idea he'd ever had.

Because no matter what she said, Walker knew the truth. Dane and Joy were meant for each other. Then. Now. It didn't matter. They were perfect together. They liked to joke, they watched the same shows on TV, they had the same favorite foods, they were both giving and attentive and so much better as people than he was. They could live a happy life together.

Joy Ride

That didn't mean he wouldn't miss them when they figured that out for themselves.

And the thought of getting attached to Arden only to lose her too—

No, he couldn't.

Not when he was already giving up so much.

"Can I ask you something?" The question popped out of Joy's mouth as if she hadn't quite intended to utter it out loud.

Before she could think of some decoy to offer up instead of whatever it was she was really wondering, Walker glanced over at her. "Anything. I'll tell you whatever you want to know."

"Are you and Dane together, like *together*, or do you only fool around when you're sharing women in bed?"

His muscles tensed so abruptly, they swerved onto the rumble strip at the edge of the road before he corrected their course and took their exit. "Shit, Joy…"

"You don't have to tell me. I think I already know the answer. And I can see why it wouldn't be smart to advertise your relationship given your father's views on the subject." Her grimace turned into a wide smile when she said, "I'm happy for you two, you know that, right?"

"It's not like what you're thinking." He tried to think of how best to explain.

"So you don't spend your nights sweaty and naked, making each other come so hard your balls nearly fall off?" Joy pouted. "Damn it. There goes all my decent masturbation material."

Was she trying to make him crash? "Oh, well, yeah. We do that."

"Thank God." She angled her body more toward him, a blush staining her cheeks even as she grinned.

"But I wouldn't say we're like...a couple." Walker felt weird even putting it that way. "It's more like we're partners, and we make do."

What he couldn't quite bring himself to say, because he didn't want to give her false hope or ruin Dane's chances at making a lasting bond with her, was that they weren't complete. They were a threesome looking for their third. Because the only time he'd felt like they had been whole was when they'd slept with her. Even the other women they'd shared were only a stand-in for the real thing.

It had always been about Joy.

The rest had sort of developed out of their mutual need, and now it was how they existed. They were fused together. But even a weld like the one keeping them together could be broken by something as powerful as Dane's love for Joy and now Arden as well.

Walker had been preparing to let Dane go from the instant he'd seen Joy walk in to Hot Rides holding an infant in her arms.

Dread coiling in his guts, he decelerated and coasted into the Hot Rides driveway, unsure of how they'd gotten there already. He'd been on autopilot.

"My turn to ask you something." He wasn't sure he wanted the answer he sensed was coming, but he had to know for certain.

Joy braced herself against the door then said, "Oh boy."

"Why has Dane been acting so fucking weird around me the past week? Did you two already have a talk like this?" Walker put the car in park and turned to meet her stare directly so she couldn't avoid telling him the truth even if it was about to hurt like a motherfucker.

12

Well, shit. Joy could only think of one reason why Dane would have changed how he was behaving toward Walker recently. He must have felt at least as guilty as she did.

"No, I wouldn't say we talked." She cleared her throat. "I mean, our mouths were too busy for that and I don't think either of us would have had adequate blood flow to our brains to carry on a discussion."

"I knew it." Walker nodded, neither angry nor surprised at her revelation. It kind of pissed her off that he seemed resigned. Didn't he want her at all? Not even a little?

If she'd said the same to Clive, he would have made sure she knew who she belonged to. But maybe that's why she loved Walker and Dane instead. There was no sense in denying it, not even to herself. Her feelings were stronger than ever, watching how they looked after their daughter and had crafted this entire new existence for themselves. She might not be in love with them yet...or was that again…but she knew now that her love for them would never fade or die if it hadn't by now.

"The day we took my motorcycle on her maiden voyage…" So she owed it to Walker to be totally honest. "We, uh, made a pit stop."

"And it involved fooling around, didn't it? He's guilty as fuck and terrible at hiding it."

"It was only a kiss. A hell of one, but still. Are you upset?" Joy asked quietly.

"Nah. Weren't you listening to me?" It soothed her ego a little to see his knuckles were white from clutching the steering wheel so tightly, even though they were going nowhere fast. "I figured it would happen sooner or later. To be honest, I assumed you two had snuck in a quickie. You wouldn't be the first to get it on in the woods around Hot Rides or, for that matter, in the garage itself."

"It's kind of intense being around everyone here. The chemistry between them is off the charts." Joy probably should shut her mouth, but she shifted in her seat thinking about how Quinn looked at Trevon and Devra when they were going about their business. Same for all of the trios, really. It was hot and made her long for someone to hunger for her that way just once in her life.

The thing was, the night she'd slept with Dane and Walker, and the day in the woods…well, it had seemed to her like they did crave her as badly as she did them.

Except she never would have been able to walk away.

Yet they had.

So she must have been mistaken.

Joy got out of the car and trudged toward their tiny home. Why did it have to be so damn cute and cozy, inviting her to stay longer than she should? She figured she'd need a couple of months of paychecks before she

Joy Ride

could go apartment hunting. Not one day more. Then she was moving out, on her own, and she'd do well to remember that.

Even when she was sleepy and her dreams seemed within reach.

She'd only made it a few steps along the short path from the parking area when Walker appeared by her side, with a steadying grip on her elbow.

"Not so fast...why *didn't* you two get it on that day?" Walker grimaced. "Other than the fact that it had to have been freezing out there. If it had been me with you—"

"Then what?" Joy couldn't stop the short, ironic laugh that burst from her chest as he opened their door and ushered her inside. "Don't act like you would have gone for it when we both know you wouldn't have. You can pretend to be macho and a player with other women—shit, maybe you are—but we both know that's not how things are between us. You still see me as your bratty little sister or something."

She clomped into the bathroom and began stripping off her day-old clothes, beginning with her shirt, which she whipped over her head and dropped to the pretty antique tile floor. She needed to wash herself clean of hospital smells and the irritation seeping out of her pores now before she could lie down in Dane's bed. That and she had to get rid of the tingle of attraction she still felt for his best friend, who'd essentially brushed her off. Again.

When Walker appeared in the doorway, she squeaked and grabbed for the nearest towel. "What are you doing?"

"You don't get to fling accusations like that then flounce away." Walker stepped closer until he towered over her. Despite her discomfort around other men, she didn't shy away or experience the slightest sliver of fear even when he was clearly agitated.

"I'll do whatever the hell I like. But at this point, fine. I don't give a fuck if you stand there." She shrugged. That caused the edge of her towel to slip, revealing one of her currently enhanced breasts. Her rack looked pretty great these days, if she did say so herself. A win for bottle-feeding breast milk.

"Joy..." He squeezed past her in the tight space to turn on the faucet in the freestanding antique bathtub, her favorite extravagance in the tiny home. "First of all, you're so tired you're likely to fall asleep in there and drown. Dane would never forgive me."

Joy glanced around. She wasn't surprised to find that the guys didn't stock any bubble bath she could at least use to obscure most of her body from him. It was probably because she was punchy with exhaustion that she thought it was a good idea, but she decided that if he was so damn indifferent and blasé about her anyway, she might as well push his previous claims and prove, once and for all, that she was right.

He was unaffected by her as a woman. Hell, maybe even repulsed.

She just wished she knew if it was because of what he'd obviously never been able to unsee from the night Clive had attacked her or because he still thought of her as a relative. Or simply because she wasn't his type.

At least on the outside, she didn't have a lot in common with the high-maintenance, sky-high-heel-wearing, ruby-red-lipped blondes he seemed to prefer. Deep down, she had believed they craved the same things.

Especially the one time he'd given in and shown her exactly how compatible they truly were.

Joy Ride

So fuck him. She was getting in that bathtub, and if he didn't care for her stretch marks or thick thighs, he would scurry away faster, leaving her to bask in the solitude and steam.

Joy dropped the towel and stared directly into his eyes as she unbuttoned her jeans and peeled them down her legs. Her underwear followed next. And if the rumors she'd heard about him in the Wildfire clubhouse were true, she taunted him most of all by turning around, daring him to avoid looking at her bare ass while she swept her hair off her shoulders.

"If you insist on staying, at least make yourself helpful and unhook my bra." She stared at him so she saw the instant his gaze dropped.

"Walker?" She snapped him out of his ogling. "That's not my bra."

"Sorry," he rasped, though he clearly wasn't.

The very tips of his fingers brushed her flanks on both sides as he lifted his hands. Despite her tremor when she shivered, he undid the garment and slid the straps down her shoulders in a single fluid motion that spoke to how practiced he was at doing it.

Joy tried not to be jealous, but she couldn't quite manage that much grace.

She let the nursing bra fall near her toes, wishing she'd had on something sexy and lacy instead. But fuck it, this was who she was and if he didn't like it, he could go like she expected him to any second.

Except he didn't.

When she turned to step into the tub, she caught sight of Walker licking his lips in her peripheral vision. Then he was there, putting his arm around her to lower her into the warm water. The strong, steady band of his muscles hugging her did nothing to douse the sparks threatening to ignite between them.

Walker knelt at the side of the tub. He put his hand under her chin and applied gentle pressure until she faced him. "Don't tempt me, Joy. It's hard enough to be around you all the time and keep my hands to myself, but if you're going to challenge how I feel about you and expect me to have enough self-control to do the right thing, I think we're both going to be disappointed in me again."

Joy swallowed hard. Things were pretty decent in general. The temporary hands-off truce they'd somehow all fallen into—her, Walker, and Dane—was working. They were living together and making it work. She would be a fool to jeopardize that.

Fine, she was a horny fool. A lonely one, too.

"Making love with you could never be a letdown," Joy said quietly. "I can still feel your touch burned onto my skin like a brand. I miss it. I miss you. Shouldn't I be the one who gets to decide what's right for me, not you? Or Dane for that matter? And certainly not Clive."

That did it. Comparing him to that monster seemed laughable to her but obviously hit home for Walker. He would never take her choices away—at least not when it came to physical intimacy—the way Clive had. But what about the rest?

Would he let her have her way?

"Fuck. Joy." He groaned, then reached for her. He took her into his arms, instantly making everything else fade away. They pressed together at their shoulders, the wall of the tub between their lower bodies. Water splashed onto the floor and across his shirt, making it stick to his pecs so that he looked like a superhero action figure.

Joy crushed herself to him, afraid of leaving even a millimeter of space between them for him to change his mind. She slid her fingers through the sides of his beard, loving the way the coarse hair abraded her skin.

She would have fisted it to hold him still as she advanced, but she didn't need to.

Walker came to her.

He took the lead, turning aggressive and possessive all at once. Where kissing Dane had been wild yet playful, making out with Walker was serious business. He parted her lips and licked her, letting her know he was there and not planning to leave anytime soon.

Hopefully.

Joy hated the whimper that escaped her throat as he plundered her breath like a pirate who stole kisses. Her hands ran down his neck and onto his shoulders, where her fingers kneaded the pads of muscle that bulged as he held her even tighter.

Her nails dug in and he cursed before kissing her with so much passion that she realized precisely how wrong she'd been.

Walker needed her like she needed him. Fuck him for hiding it for so long.

The fact that he'd been willing to sacrifice his chance to do this with her every day for the rest of their lives meant he truly loved her, and Dane. He'd been prepared to forsake the most incredible rush she'd ever experienced to make them happy.

Okay, now she might be in danger of falling in love with the thickskulled, sexy, alpha man.

And that was much more dangerous than the potential for drowning.

Joy pushed away from him, struggling to catch her

breath. He stared at her, the tendons in his neck standing out as he gulped in air of his own.

Walker balled his fists, staring at the water swirling around her calves as she sat—her feet flat on the bottom of the tub, her knees bent. Silence stretched between them. Then he retrieved a clean washcloth from the cabinet beneath the sink and proceeded to lather it with soap.

He started at her toes, plucking one foot from the bath and massaging her muscles while cleaning her skin. The water rose and rose along with her desire as he worked his way up her legs. He paused before dipping between her thighs and cleaning her pussy.

Joy couldn't hold back a sigh at the contact of his soapy hand. She collapsed against the back of the tub, spreading her legs for him and wishing he had more in mind than cleaning her body. He didn't take the opening, though, instead proceeding to tend to every inch of her stomach then upward. He paid special attention to her breasts.

She closed her eyes, in no danger of drifting off now. Joy was far too excited to fall asleep and miss out on whatever he planned to do with her next.

Truth was, whatever it was, she wasn't about to stop him.

Walker could have all of her if he wanted it.

Please, let him want it.

He wrung out the cloth, then tapped her shoulder. "Come over here. Spin this way so I can wash your hair."

"Is that all?" She hated that she'd asked.

"For now." He used a glass from the sink and filled it with fresh water before pouring it over her hair. She closed her eyes again, tipping her head back to keep it out of her face.

Walker's lips brushed her forehead a moment before he dispensed shampoo into his hands and began to work it into her hair, making sure to massage her scalp. Her toes curled where she braced them on the opposite side of the tub, and she thought she might melt or maybe purr.

It surprised her again, this tender side of him he never showed the world. How deep had he buried it within himself? Had growing up with Wildfire done that to him?

She hated the club even more than she already did.

Too soon, he rinsed the bubbles from her hair, yet neither of them moved to get her out of the tub. He leaned down and whispered in her ear, "I should put you to bed."

"Yes, you definitely should."

"Alone, I mean." He cursed then as her stomach dropped to her toes. "Don't worry, Joy. I can't do it. I can't let you go without at least a taste of you."

13

Joy did her best to keep from bursting into tears. She'd been sure Walker was about to leave her with a mass of pent-up passion and nothing to do with it. But he didn't. Not entirely.

He spun her around and plucked her from the bathwater as if she weighed as much as Devra or maybe Arden, even though she'd never been petite. He perched her ass on the edge of the tub and left her legs to dangle outside of it, dripping water all over his pretty tile.

Instinctively, she reached behind her, using an arm to brace herself on the opposite side.

One of Walker's was around her waist and his other hand rested on her thigh. He stared at her pussy, pink and wet from the warm water, and hummed.

Walker dipped his head. "Joy? Is this okay?" He hesitated with his mouth a fraction of an inch from her flesh.

"It will be if you come a little closer. Don't stop now or I swear I'll die." She reached for him with her free hand. "I'm pretty sure Dane won't care if we…you know."

"He won't, though if I was as decent as him I would walk away and leave you to him. What I meant was, I don't know anything about having kids and how long you have to wait after and stuff like that. I'm not going to hurt you, am I?" He brushed his thumbs over her folds as if she was a dessert he was dying to sample, if only he wasn't allergic to it or some shit.

"Oh, no." She stroked his hair and nudged his head closer to her core. "I was evaluated at Arden's visits. I was cleared for sex weeks ago."

"Great. Hold on." He didn't give her more warning than that before burying his face between her legs.

She wasn't sure what to grab, him or the tub, so she did both. Her right hand hooked around the back of his neck while the other still clung to the rounded porcelain behind her. Walker took care of the rest.

He started lightly using the flat of his tongue, laving her pussy with long laps that had her ass lifting. She put one foot on either side of him and arched so he had full access to her most intimate parts.

Walker took the opportunity to cup her ass, holding her to his mouth and lessening the burden on the straight-locked arm behind her. He was so fucking strong, she knew he'd never let her fall. Her body, at least, was safe with him.

Her heart and soul were two entirely different matters.

There would be time to worry about those later.

Joy's head dropped back and she moaned when he burrowed deeper and began to suck on her clit with light and frequent pulses. The man might not know about maternity issues, but he sure as fuck knew how to bring a woman pleasure. "Walker!"

He growled as he repeated whatever the hell he'd

done to zap electricity along her nerve endings. Over and over until she wailed and shuddered. And right when she thought she couldn't take anymore, he scooted his thumb from beneath her leg to her opening and pressed it the barest bit inside.

Her pussy clung to him as he inserted his digit and used it to draw circles that stroked all of her most sensitive places from within. He was so much better than even her favorite vibrator. She couldn't imagine how good it would be once he used his dick.

Okay, yes, she could. Because he'd done it to her before and she'd fucking loved every second of it.

That thought alone propelled her toward the edge. He looked up at her as he ate her, the intensity in his dark eyes encouraging her to fly. He wanted her to come all over his face and she wasn't about to let him down.

Joy tensed, her entire body straining to be closer to Walker and the incredible things he made her feel. Her heart raced and her pussy tightened. Walker's fingers dug into her, only adding to the impressions he left on her.

She lost it.

Despite wanting to cling to the livewire of ecstasy for the rest of her life, it burned too bright and set her soul on fire. Joy met Walker's stare as she exploded, riding his face as he redoubled his efforts, prolonging her rapture for far longer than she would have thought possible.

And when she spasmed, he wrapped her in his arms and drew her to his chest, keeping her from breaking her skull open in the process. That was good, because she had absolutely no control over her body. He had it all.

Walker cradled her on his lap as he sat on his heels on the hard floor. He held her close, rocking slightly, and whispered in her ear, "You're so fucking beautiful. Always, but especially when you come for me."

There was nothing she could say to that so she didn't even try, but she tucked the compliment deep into her heart, a memory she would treasure for the rest of her life, no matter what else happened between them.

Walker reached to the side and grabbed a towel, using it to carefully mop every last drop of water from her as she floated in the bliss he'd generated within her. She was still having trouble returning to reality when he stood, lifting her.

He carried her the short walk to Dane's room, where she and Arden were staying, and laid her on the bed. Joy scooted over to make room for him, but he shook his head.

"What?" she asked. "You're not joining me?"

"No, you need to sleep, not expend more energy." Instead of following her down, blanketing her with his body, and making love to her until they both passed out, he pulled the soft sheet and fluffy comforter over her, tucking her in.

She stared at the raging erection stretching along his thigh beneath his now too-tight jeans. He wanted her. Like always, that didn't mean he was going to do anything about it.

"A hard-on never killed anybody." He shrugged. "I've got a hand. It'll be fine."

"If you don't want to..." Her voice hitched as inside she thought *want me*. "I get it. But will you at least lay here and hold me. Stay with me, please."

"I can't, Joy. And now you know why." He scrubbed his hands over his face. "It's all I can do to resist you. It's always been that way."

Joy Ride

With her safely mummified in the covers, he sat on the edge of the bed and took her hand in his. Part of her wanted to snatch it back, but it turned out, she couldn't do it either.

"These issues between us. The tension. It was never about you, Joy. It's about me." He sighed. "Yeah, at first I thought I was going straight to hell for lusting after my sister. But pretty quick it was more than that. You were Dane's. And club rules say... Fuck that. My own screwed-up morals say that means you're off limits. And then the shit with Clive went down and I was ashamed."

"Of me? Of the fact that everyone knew what he'd taken from me?" Her eyes went unfocused, and in the blur the only thing she could see was the ceiling of her old room in Walker's father's house. Clive's grunts and her own sobs echoed in her ears.

"Never!" Walker's rage drew her back to the present. "You should know that I intended to kill him. It was only Dane, and his commitment to the recruiter, the contract we signed saying we'd go, that kept me from executing my plan. Executing him. My father knew and was fine with it, by the way. He told me I should do what had to be done. To fight for my woman. Except I knew then, like I know now, that you were never meant to be mine, Joy. You were meant to be Dane's. He saved my life. Kept me from taking a fucked-up situation and making it worse. Going down a path I could never come back from. You and he were the ones who suffered most, and I made it even harder on you both. I took him from you. He went to save me. That's the truth."

Walker shot to his feet then, dropping her hand to the mattress.

She'd never seen him so tormented before, his emotions so close to the surface.

Joy pushed herself to her elbows, but she was too damn weary to go farther than that. Not only because of what she'd been through in the past twenty-four hours, but because of what life had thrown at them for the past decade. It hit her all at once.

"Walker," she said softly. "That was then. This is now. We're different people. Why don't we start over?"

"It would be nice if I could erase my sins with a snap of my fingers. This shit is tangled up in my mind. And I still think that Dane is your best bet. He can be the kind of man you need, the father Arden deserves. It's him. Not me. And I should have thought about that before I almost let us get carried away." His right hand balled into a fist and he punched his left palm. "I'm sorry. I shouldn't have done that."

"You think I'm weak. That I can't handle myself."

"Are you listening? It's me who's fucked up. You're perfect. I'm too rough for a woman like you. Anyone decent, really." He shook his head and crossed to the door. "And that includes Dane. I want you to know that I haven't touched him since you came back into our lives. *His* life. He's yours."

He held his hands up, palms open, as if he was letting go and giving her another person. As if Dane didn't have any say in the matter, just like she hadn't.

Walker was absolutely infuriating. Or would be if she wasn't too worn down to fight back.

Joy let herself fall. She crashed to the fluffy pillow that still smelled like Dane and buried her face in it. She wished he were there right then to make sense of everything that was going on.

Joy Ride

It surprised her when Walker didn't leave and instead inched near her again. He leaned down and kissed the tip of her nose. "You should talk to Dane about this stuff. He's always been the right guy for you and he still is. Even more importantly, he's the right man to be a father to Arden. The best. Don't tempt me, Joy. That's not some kind of threat. That's me begging. Please. I can't say no to you any more than I can to him."

"Looks like you just did, asshole."

"I told you. I'm the worst." Walker huffed as he spun on his heel and made his way toward the room he was sharing with Dane. "Sleep well, Joy. I'll be out here making sure you're safe. And when you wake up, we'll go get your daughter."

"Our daughter," she mumbled.

He said something low, but it was garbled and she was fading fast. It almost sounded like, "If only I were so lucky."

But he might be. Why couldn't he believe it?

Before she could ask, he left her by herself. Again.

If she heard one peep from the other side of the wall, a single moan or sigh that made it sound like Walker was getting off without her, she was going to cannonball into his bed and force him to allow her to relieve the pressure that kept building day after tortuous day, even if it meant demeaning herself by pleading.

Whether he realized it or not, Walker needed Dane. And he might even need her.

He was unraveling. Or maybe that was simply his true personality emerging from the stranglehold the Wildfire environment had put on him since he was a child.

It wasn't often she saw this side of him, though she'd glimpsed it more often since she'd come to Hot Rides than at any other time in his life. He was mellowing out, maturing even. Maybe settling down. Letting himself be vulnerable to his own emotions.

That freaked her out some, because if that was true and he still wanted nothing to do with her, it meant the problem probably wasn't him.

It could be her. Maybe they simply weren't compatible, like he said.

She wondered what Dane would have to say about that. As soon as she'd slept and was back on top of her game, she was going to ask him point blank.

Joy let her eyes drift closed so that she could dream about the things she wished were possible. This new Walker, one she hadn't been privy to in the past, was even more seductive than his dominant, give-no-fucks, bad boy counterpart.

He was a warrior. That she'd always known.

But he was also a lover. A caretaker. And discovering that now might be incredibly hazardous. Because it made her long for things she'd given up on a decade ago.

Things that had more to do with her heart than the tingles between her legs, which her orgasm—as intense as it had been—hadn't even come close to soothing.

Joy needed much more than a single epic climax from Walker, and Dane, to be satisfied.

14

Dane rode bitch on the couch that had seemed plenty roomy when it had been only him and Walker lounging on it. All of a sudden, now that he was plunked right in between Joy and his best friend, it suddenly seemed like he didn't have enough room to breathe, let alone get comfortable.

Sitting this close to them, his thighs touching each of them, he felt torn apart.

He loved Joy.

Always had. And after tasting her the other day he felt guiltier than ever about how desperately he wanted her. Worse, his feelings for Walker hadn't changed either. If he didn't have the guy in his life, never mind his bed, it would be worse than never riding a motorcycle again.

It would fundamentally change who he was.

So what the hell was he going to do?

Something had to give. Being stuck in the middle had already changed him. For example, he hadn't told Walker what went down during the test drive of Joy's bike.

If he told Walker about what had happened in the

woods, about how he'd let his guard down and put Joy at risk, he knew he'd get the beating he deserved. That was the Wildfire way and they hadn't entirely grown out of those bad habits, had they?

That was the entire problem. They'd been making progress...

Yet it seemed like Walker had taken some enormous steps backward from his mindset on New Year's Eve. He'd definitely not said another peep about pursuing a committed relationship together, despite the perfect opportunity that had presented itself.

Could it be that despite everything he said, Walker still wished he could have Joy, and have her to himself?

Dane looked from Joy to Walker and back. Neither of them had come clean about it, but he could tell something had happened between them, too. He tried to snuff out the jealousy rearing its ugly head but couldn't do it. Not this time.

He'd ignored the attraction between those two when they'd been kids and he hadn't known how to handle it. But now...

He might let Walker fuck him, but that didn't mean he'd allow the guy to walk all over him or decide what was best for the three of them when his choices were obviously making everyone miserable.

In full view of Walker, he laid his hand possessively on Joy's thigh. She didn't retreat, not that there was a lot of room to scooch over since she was already plastered to the arm of the couch. The stare she leveled at him was almost a dare. One he planned to accept. It would kill him to do otherwise.

"What are you doing?" she asked quietly.

"Being stupid again, probably." He swallowed hard.

"But it's driving me crazy to be this close to you without doing something about it."

Dane hoped Walker realized that he'd meant both of them when he said *you*.

Joy still didn't get up and run away.

So he turned his upper body to the side and lifted his hands to frame either side of her face. Her eyes were warm and soft as they flicked downward, her gaze landing on his open mouth. At least this time, if they got carried away, Walker would be there to watch their backs. The guy always did.

With that weight lifted off Dane's shoulders, he leaned in and slanted his mouth over Joy's.

She parted her lips, letting him in like she always had. One taste and he was a goner. He never could get enough of her. The mint of her toothpaste, her heat and softness. The sound of her breathing growing ragged. It was appealing to all of his senses.

Walker's too, apparently. "Yeah, that's it. Fucking kiss her, Dane. Show her how much you missed her. Did you tell her that you were coming to get her if she hadn't found us first?"

"Wait..." Joy broke them apart, using her palms on his chest for leverage. "What? You were?"

Dane could hardly think, but he nodded and groaned. "Yes."

She whipped her gaze to Walker then, but the other man was saved from answering her unspoken questions, because right then the baby wailed.

Walker stood up so fast the entire couch rocked onto two legs then landed with a thud that shook the floor. Arden, who'd been napping in Dane's old room—now home to Joy and Arden—screamed louder.

"I've got her," Walker said, and before Joy or Dane could object, he was stumbling toward the other room.

Dane and Joy sat face to face, breathing hard for long enough that Walker's deep, soothing croons worked on them nearly as well as Arden. Except, when he'd settled the baby and emerged from the bedroom, he didn't look like he planned to return to his spot.

The pink diaper bag dangling from his shoulder in no way made him look less intimidating or manly. In fact, it only emphasized how muscular he was, since it looked miniscule on him compared to when Joy hauled the thing around.

He grabbed a bottle out of the refrigerator, then zipped Arden into her fleece coveralls, the ones with the cute bear ears on the hood. "I'm taking her to the garage with me. I won't be back for...a while. You two have fun."

"You're sure this is how you want to do this?" Joy stood and faced him.

"Certain." Walker gave a single nod, then tipped Arden toward Joy for a moment. "Say bye to Mommy. Tell her we're going to play with our friends and she should too."

Joy couldn't resist going close enough to kiss Arden on forehead and fuss with her clothes before taking a huge breath and then stepping back. "You know how I feel about this. I'm not kicking you out, but I'm also not going to say no."

"Good." Walker put one arm around her and squeezed Joy tight before letting go. Dane knew that if he held her for any longer than that, he wouldn't be able to walk out the door.

So why was he going at all?

"Wouldn't you rather stay?" Dane asked the man.

Walker paused with his hand on the doorknob. He looked over his shoulder, his eyes swimming with regret. "That's not how this was meant to be. For once in my life, I'm going to do the right thing. You should too, even though our paths are diverging. It's okay, Dane."

Then he drew Arden's hood up, tucked her close to his chest to block as much of the cold wind as possible from blasting her, and took off toward Hot Rides. He was halfway to the garage before Dane could even consider chasing after him to argue. He bolted from the couch. "I should..."

Joy put her hand on his upper arm, stopping him with the slightest of touches. "He's a grown man, responsible for his own choices. So are you. Are you going to blow your chance with me, too?"

Dane looked out the window a moment longer before turning back to Joy. "No. I don't plan to. But I can't figure out what I'm supposed to do. He and I have been a team for so long, especially in bed. It's weird and I feel bad."

"Why? He didn't when he went down on me the other day." Joy shrugged.

"He what?" Dane's eyes widened. He figured they'd made out like he and Joy had. Figures Walker had gone further—he was bolder than Dane ever could be. Story of their lives, really.

"I'm sorry. I should have told you right away." The corners of Joy's eyes pinched and her forehead creased. "I hope that doesn't piss you off."

"I mean, if it does, it's only because I missed it. Where the hell was I?" Dane sure as shit would have heard it if he'd been home. Walker knew how to get a woman off, hard, and Joy wasn't shy when it came to enjoying their attention. The night they'd shared her, she'd been so affectionate, giving, and sensual.

His cock stiffened thinking about it. And just like that, he was finding it hard to concentrate on anything other than finally being with Joy. The two of them, spending as much time as they liked exploring each other and simply enjoying the effect their touches, kisses, and whatever else would have.

"You were at Hot Rods with Arden when Walker brought me home from the hospital. We didn't plan for it to happen…"

"I get it. I feel the same way when I'm around you." Dane caressed her cheek with the backs of his knuckles. "I don't blame him. Or you. It's hard to resist either of you."

"Should we go get him?" Joy asked.

Dane shook his head. "Fuck it. I don't want to be talked out of this right now. Or let the universe put some new roadblock in our way. I need you, Joy. I always have. I'm going to take his bait. If that makes me a shitty man, so be it."

She bit her lip, then nodded. "I agree. We can fix things with Walker later, right?"

"I hope so. But if not, you'll have me. I swear I'm never going to leave your side again. I shouldn't have done it before. Not the first time or the second time and definitely not the third time. It ripped my heart out to leave you lying naked in that bed." He would grovel if he had to. "I hope you know I only did it because it seemed wise at the time. I had nothing to offer you."

"So make it up to me now," Joy said with a smile that was equal parts coy and devilish before unwrapping the shawl she'd had on over her tank top, which left her breasts easy to access for pumping.

Dane thought he might be experiencing a full-on feeding frenzy of his own soon enough. She looked so mature, her breasts ripe and full, reminding him of how well she provided for their daughter.

Joy was incredible. And he couldn't wait to show her what a goddess she was to him.

He took her hand and intertwined their fingers, like they used to when they would sneak away for long walks in the woods near the Wildfire clubhouse, which weren't all that different from where they'd made out the other day. Except back then his kisses had been chaste and now they were anything but.

Dane used their connection to draw her into their room, then shut the door softly behind them and locked it, keeping everyone else out but them. Their mountain of troubles and the rest of the world didn't matter. At least for the next couple of hours.

He put his palm on the wood and slowly counted to five, but there was no turning back now.

When he spun to face Joy and saw her staring back at him with wide eyes, he drew his shirt over his head, leaving himself bare-chested and bare-footed. His hands dropped to the button of his jeans. There was no use in denying this interlude between them would end any way except with them naked.

"Hold on..." Joy hesitated, covering the evidence of her hardened nipples with one hand. Her breasts spilled over her palm, enticing him even more. He adored the changes in her that motherhood had wrought both on her body and on her spirit. She was protective, fierce, tough, and nurturing.

Dane licked his lips, imagining what it would be like to kiss and fondle them.

"Up here." She drew his attention to her gaze, which was surprisingly candid and vulnerable. Not at all like the Joy he knew, who was a survivor—tough enough on her own but not afraid to rely on bravado when her courage fell short. Today was different. It could change their whole lives if he wasn't careful with the real woman beneath the armor she too-often donned.

"You okay?" he wondered.

"I will be. It's just...you're not planning to leave me behind again, right? If we do this, where will we stand later? Whose bed are you going to sleep in tonight?" Joy scrunched her eyes closed. "Never mind. I shouldn't have asked. I don't care. I want to do this regardless of what comes next."

She reached for him and Dane didn't dare take even a single step back. He strode into her embrace and smothered her in his own. "I'm not going anywhere, Joy, I swear. I'm here and I'm yours for as long as you'll have me. Even if you deserve so much more. I can't fight it anymore."

A solitary tear ran down her cheek and he leaned in to kiss it away.

"I'm sorry for anything I've ever done—or didn't do—that's hurt you," Dane whispered. "I can't take that shit back, but I'll do my best to make up for it now. And try not to do it again in the future."

"That's good enough for me." Joy opened her eyes, which sparkled with the rest of her unshed tears. "Same goes."

"I guess I'll have to improve myself instead of hoping you find someone better." Dane wasn't bullshitting her. He intended to do everything in his power to provide for her and Arden—financially and emotionally—to be a positive influence in their lives, and to earn every bit of affection they gave him.

"I like that plan. Nobody's perfect, Dane." She winced.

"Lies," he whispered before kissing her lightly, getting off on her bare arms touching the skin of his back as she hugged him while he did it. "You are. You always have been to me."

She laughed at that, though it wasn't a humorous sort of chuckle. "Sure. I'm damaged goods. Struggling to get by. And I'm such a slut, I don't even know who the father of my baby is. I'm practically saint material."

"Lucky for you, I prefer bad girls anyway." Dane tucked a stray lock of hair behind her ear.

"And bad boys, apparently." One corner of her mouth cocked up as she teased him.

The fact that she didn't seem to mind whatever nontraditional relationship he'd fallen into with Walker only made him twice as hard. He couldn't wait a moment longer to kiss her properly.

15

Dane buried the fingers of one hand in Joy's hair. He held her head steady as he dipped his head and took her mouth with his own. The full body shudder that raced through her at their initial contact only enhanced his own reactions.

His cock strained against his jeans, eager to follow through on the promises his lips were making while his pulse pounded in his neck and wrists as if he'd already started the strenuous activity that was about to follow.

Dane schooled himself to take things slow. To savor each and every brush of his tongue against hers. He'd dreamed about this opportunity and now that he had it, he wasn't going to waste an instant by failing to appreciate how incredible Joy made him feel.

And, hopefully, how he could do the same for her.

She sighed and went pliant in his arms, giving in to this softer side of herself he'd only ever glimpsed during intimate moments. That someone like her would put that much faith in him, made him feel like he could lift his chopper over his head with one hand and twirl it around his fingertip like a basketball.

Walker did that for him too. One of the reasons they'd stuck together so long.

They brought out the best parts of each other.

Except…well, let's be honest. Walker didn't have one of Dane's favorite things…boobs.

As they made out his hands wandered, skimming beneath the hem of her tank, then walking them up her slightly more rounded belly. She squirmed as if she was uncomfortable with him revealing that part of her and the stretch marks that hadn't been there last year, when she'd previously exposed this much of herself to him.

"You have nothing to hide from me," he promised. "I love that you carried our child. It makes me want you that much more, and I already thought it would be impossible to think of you more highly than I did. This was something I never dared hope for."

Joy nodded as if she couldn't speak in the face of his pure devotion. To her and to Arden.

She grabbed the shirt and ripped it from her body, allowing him to appreciate every bit of her in the golden afternoon sun. Her breasts hung lower with the increased weight, but they were so inviting he knew he had to finish the job for her or they probably wouldn't even get fully naked before he got carried away.

"Gorgeous," he murmured as he sank to his knees in order to work her cotton sweats down her legs. Then he went back and took her underwear off too.

When Joy reached for him, he let her do as she pleased, which was apparently to rid him of his jeans as well. "I want to see you too. You're so different, Dane. So much…bigger."

He couldn't help it, he cracked up.

"Not that." She laughed too, easing some of the tension when she lightly smacked his abs. "Just... everywhere. You're not a kid anymore. Walker was always kind of built, but you...*damn*. I didn't have the chance to admire you properly when we did this before."

She ran her fingers along his biceps then down his pecs and along the ridges of his abs.

Joy didn't stop there. She paid special attention to the crease that led from his hip toward his dick first with her inquisitive touch and then with her mouth, licking and kissing her way closer to her goal above the waistband of his low-riding jeans.

He did his best to stand still and let her take anything she needed.

Even when she carefully lowered the zipper on his pants and shoved the fabric from his hips.

"Okay. Maybe that too." Joy purred as she cupped his cock, measuring him. This was about as far as they'd ever made it when they were younger, though with their clothes still on. Still, her touch was familiar and it reminded him of the times she'd perched him right on the edge of orgasm with a simple grope or two when no one was looking.

Then again, he'd been young and had no stamina. These days he could do a hell of a lot better.

Dane put his hands on Joy's shoulders and walked her backward until the side of the bed impressed on her calves. Then he guided her down, supporting her when she otherwise would have toppled, bouncing onto the ultra-comfortable foam mattress he and Walker had sprung for once they'd built up some savings.

It was nice to be able to provide a few creature

comforts for themselves and, now, for Joy. He crawled onto the bed after her, lowering himself bit by bit to make sure he never saw even a hint of fear in her eyes or the way she held her body.

Joy put her arms up and welcomed him into her personal space so he went, ending up with his face nuzzled in her cleavage.

She laughed again, the lyrical quality of her happiness like music to his ears. He could already tell that sex with her was going to be fun. Playful. All the things that sex with Walker wasn't.

Then Joy hesitated. "Dane, you realize that could get messy, right?"

"Does it bother you if it does?" He caressed the sides of her breasts as lightly as he could, angling his face to carefully monitor her expression.

She moaned softly then said, "Not if you're okay with it."

"It's fine. Natural. But does this still feel good?"

"Honestly, it's even better than before. I'm so... sensitive. Be gentle though, please?" She arched her back, presenting her chest to him.

"That I can do." He kissed her neck and then her collarbones and finally her breasts. He took his time, testing the effects of light glancing touches, tender kisses, and then the barest bit of sucking. At that, Joy twitched and moaned, so he continued, repeating the motion over and over.

He rocked against her as he did, his cock gliding through the precome that had leaked from the tip as he feasted on her. And when Joy realized what he was doing, she lent a hand. Literally. Her fingers wormed between them to encircle his shaft.

Joy Ride

She wrapped him in her palm and used her fingers to massage him as he slid through her grip while devouring her. Joy jerked him off—slowly and with so much more finesse than Walker did when he was fucking Dane. Her strokes were gentle and languid, and a little too light to be too dangerous to his self-control, which was a plus.

It gave him plenty of time to explore her body and find the places that made her inhale sharply or wriggle on the bed beneath him. She was so easy to please, so open with her reactions, it made it all the more enjoyable to tease her.

To be honest, he could have done it endlessly, watching the color rise up her chest and stain her cheeks. But eventually Joy got restless. She obviously needed more than his peripheral caresses.

Reluctantly, Dane placed a final lingering kiss on each of her breasts then shifted so that their bodies were better aligned. His cock slipped from her fingers, making him groan.

"Why don't you put that somewhere more appropriate?" she joked with a sassy grin that made his heart clench in his chest.

"I liked it just fine where it was." He kissed the tip of her nose. Hopefully she didn't think that just because he and Walker were far more experienced than she was that he'd forgotten how to enjoy simple pleasures. Besides, with her, everything felt new and exciting.

More intense.

Because with her, it meant something more than a physical release. While he'd had that with Walker—in their own way—he'd never experienced it openly or with a woman before.

He must have hovered there, staring into her pretty

eyes for long enough to give her the wrong impression. To make her think that he might not be about to join them together.

"Dane, I need you inside me." She reached for him, but he had to do it himself. To show her how deeply he desired her. He didn't have to be coaxed. This was his wish as much as hers.

He evaded her by settling deeper between her spread legs, letting his cock rest on her mound, giving her plenty of time to change her mind, though she didn't. Dane rode the furrow of her pussy, coating himself with the ample lubrication on her flesh.

The last thing he wanted was to cause her even the slightest bit of discomfort. Especially now that he knew how innocent she truly was. They had probably been far too rough with her that night they'd thought they were saying goodbye forever. But she hadn't seemed to mind.

What they shared now was something entirely different without the desperation and regret, the fear and the pain. This was pure bliss. An expression of a decade of pent-up attraction and, yes, lust.

"You're positive?" he asked.

"I've never been more sure about something in my life." She wrapped her arms around him and smothered him in her loving embrace.

It was irresistible.

Dane took his dick in hand and guided it to Joy's body. Her skin was warm and soft and wet and impossible to back away from. He inched closer, inserting the head just enough to keep him in place before propping himself up on his elbows.

Holding himself above Joy, he looked deep into her eyes. "Is this really what you want? Am *I* what you need?"

"Hell yes." She wrapped her legs around his hips and her arms around his neck, then used her limbs to pull him in. His cock burrowed deeper within the grasp of her hot pussy.

He fit there like he belonged. Because he did.

"Joy," he moaned, and buried his face in the crook of her neck, kissing and licking the delicate spot beneath her ear until she relaxed around him, allowing him to fuse them more completely.

"Yes," she sighed, and arched, trying to take more of him.

"You have no idea how many times I imagined this moment," Dane murmured as he brushed the hair from her face. "I'm so sorry it wasn't me who got to do this with you the first time. To do it right. I will never forgive myself for that."

His cock lost some of its rigidity.

"It's about time you did, Dane." Joy kissed him gently as her hands ran down his back and flank then back up again, petting him, soothing him. "Because I've never held you at fault. There was only one person responsible that night. It took me years to realize it wasn't me."

"It wasn't, you know that, right?" Dane paused to kiss her, wishing he could do more.

"I do. And it certainly wasn't you. So make it right now. Make us whole again. Put things back the way they should always have been. Don't let him take this from us too."

There wasn't a chance he could resist her pleas when that was exactly what he wished for too.

Dane dropped his face to hers and kissed her as he rubbed up against her. And when his cock had gotten back onboard, he pressed forward again, sinking deeper.

They came together bit by bit until his erection was nestled fully within her.

"Damn, Joy." He breathed against her lips before flexing his hips, grinding their bodies together as if he could make them any closer than they already were. The motion must have rubbed her clit just the right way, because she moaned.

"Do that again," she sighed.

It was odd, fucking in slow motion. So different from anything he'd ever experienced before. Some kind of tantric glide that was more about how fully they could connect than how often he could leave her body simply to return again.

Pistoning in and out of her, riding her in some sexual frenzy, wasn't what either of them craved. This was the bawdy version of a joy ride. Leisurely. Prolonged. Undertaken for the pure pleasure of the experience itself rather than as a way to get from Point A to Point B.

With Joy, that's all he needed to get off and get off hard.

He would rather make love like this for the whole day, staying intimately joined, than fuck her fast and hard so they were done in a flash. It was pretty much the complete opposite of how things were when he was with Walker.

His ass clenched as he thought of the stuff they'd done together in the middle of the night. That only embedded his cock deeper in Joy.

Maybe he needed both kinds of loving. Maybe he always had. Could that be why he'd hesitated with Joy when they were younger? Because he'd known something was missing?

Last time the three of them had slept together—the only time—he and Walker had focused on Joy. What would it be like if Walker stormed into the bedroom right then, came up behind him, and drilled deep into Dane's ass? What if he fucked Dane while Dane rode Joy?

His cock jerked within her.

"I have no idea what you're doing, but it feels incredible. Do it again." Joy threw her head back, exposing her neck to him. So he did while kissing the pale column.

Over and over.

As he made love to her, her body told him how much she enjoyed it. She tightened around him like a slippery fist. Only pure determination kept him from exploding within her when she tumbled over the edge into climax the first time, shuddering then clenching around him with rhythmic pulses designed to draw the come straight from his balls.

Although he slowed, he kept moving throughout her climax, stoking the embers of her arousal until she began to climb again. "Oh shit, Dane. You're going to make me come more if you keep doing that."

"That's the point." He grinned before he kissed her, nibbling on her lower lip as she began to spiral higher.

They didn't talk after that and his errant thoughts drifted away as he concentrated on chasing the feelings that only she could instill in him. It was indulgent, decadent, and made up for a tiny bit of the time they'd been forced to spend apart.

He never wanted to leave her now that they'd found each other once more.

Dane felt like he'd been pumping into her for hours. Hell, maybe he had been. His mind had blanked and all he could do was rock into her like a pendulum on a clock, erasing the moments they'd lost, filling her exactly how she responded to loudest. She had long ago stopped verbalizing her demands but instead showed him with her body exactly how much she appreciated his marathon efforts.

Joy had climaxed at least a half dozen times and seemed to be working on another when her eyes opened and pierced into his soul. "Come with me this time. Experience what I have."

Dane nodded. It was getting nearly impossible not to flood her pussy. Sweat beaded on his brow and ran down his temples.

"How does Walker get you off?" she asked breathily, without judgment but plenty of genuine curiosity.

"Usually he jerks me off while he fucks me." Dane was too far gone to hedge. He blurted out the truth, a spurt of precome leaking from him in response.

"You like having him in your ass?"

He nodded, his balls drawing up tight to his torso as he thought about it. Too horny to be ashamed of the truth.

"But we've never done that when we share women." Dane admitted. "Usually he fucks their ass and I fuck their pussy and they…"

"Get the ride of their lives." Joy grinned, except her amusement faded after a second. "But what about you, Dane? Do you have what you need?"

"This is everything," he said reflexively.

"I'm not sure." She hesitated for the first time that afternoon, though her pussy was squeezing him harder, rippling around him faintly as it did right before she came. It caught him by surprise when she jammed her hand between them and worked a finger in beside his shaft, wriggling along his length and making it even more difficult to maintain his steady pace.

Joy Ride

"Oh, I'm positive." He was going to fucking lose it in her any second.

"Don't ever be afraid to tell me how to make this better for you. What you crave." She withdrew her finger, then wrapped her arm around him and slid it down the center of his back until it reached his ass.

"What are you—?" He tensed, but not enough to prevent her from hitting her target.

Her slippery finger ringed his hole before pressing against the center.

"Oh fuck." He groaned and collapsed onto Joy, probably smothering her with his weight. She didn't seem to mind. Dane kept grinding on her—afraid of dislodging her hand, which could barely reach his ass—as she impaled him.

And when she began to rub his hole from within, using the same rhythm he kept as he traced slow circles on her body, he knew their session was about to come to an end. A glorious, grand finale the likes of which he'd never experienced before.

"Joy!" he shouted.

"I'm with you," she promised.

It was the most arousing thing he'd ever heard. He had Joy. She accepted him for who he was, his past, his mistakes, and his passions.

What more could he want?

He needed for her to feel the same. And he was pretty sure she did when she began to tremble beneath him, her pussy hugging him so tight he was afraid she might leave a permanent dent in his dick.

It would be worth it if she did.

Dane stared straight into her wide-open eyes as he let himself tumble first. He trusted that she would keep her word and that she was falling too. They were in this together.

His ass clenched on her finger several times before his release poured from his dick, deep within her. Dane flooded her pussy with so much come that it squeezed out beside his dick and still he kept shooting, his orgasm extending far beyond usual.

Joy screamed and clasped him with both her legs and her free arm. She bucked, impaling herself on his cock with every subconscious flex of her body.

In that moment, Dane realized he'd been wrong about a lot of things. He'd thought he was experienced, that he'd done pretty much everything there was to do in bed, but he'd never done this…had pure, emotion-fueled sex with the woman he would love until his dying breath.

Long after his balls were empty and she'd melted beneath him, he stayed embedded within her, afraid to leave paradise now that he'd found it. They touched each other all over, with comforting strokes that mellowed them both out.

For the first time, maybe in his entire life, Dane was content.

Only when he wilted and finally slipped from her did he lean over, grab some baby wipes from Arden's changing station and take his time cleaning the fluid that had been expressed from her breasts, and the rest of their bodies. Proof of the impact they had on each other.

The fact that Joy let him tend to her meant nearly as much as the revolutionary release they'd shared. She trusted him, and for the first time, he might be starting to believe in himself as much as she did.

Dane burrowed into his pillow and drew Joy to him, wrapping her in his arms and legs, sheltering her as much as possible with his body. He might not always be able to keep her safe from the outside world, but he swore then and there that he was done injuring her with his own insecurities.

Running away was no longer an option.

"I love you, Joy," he promised.

"I love you too." She seemed like she wanted to say more.

"But?"

"I also love Walker," Joy whispered. "What's wrong with me?"

"Whatever it is, I've got the same problem." Dane shrugged. "I'm not sure how it happened, but this is how it is now. How I am. And honestly, I think it's how Walker is too, even if he's still trying to avoid the truth."

"He tries so hard to control everything. To make the world around him behave as he thinks is best." Joy sighed. "I imagine it's difficult for him to accept a curveball like… well…whatever it is the two of you have together."

"You know, you're exactly right." Dane hadn't ever put his finger on it quite like Joy did. She saw things so clearly sometimes. "At least about his puppeteering. He's been pulling that shit forever. Hell, even when we were kids. I could tell how attracted he was to you. But instead of crossing whatever line he thought there was because your mom and his dad hooked up, he tried to push us closer together. That way he'd have another excuse to tell himself what he hungered for was wrong. I can't tell you how many times he told me back then that I should sleep with you. That you wanted to take our relationship further."

"I did." Joy proved Walker right again. "But if you didn't want the same thing…"

"What? You can't really believe that, can you?" Dane tipped her chin up so he could read the answer in her stare. She did. "I was trying to do the right thing. Let you grow up some. I figured we had plenty of time to get more serious. Of course, I couldn't have been more wrong about that."

"I hate to say this, but I think you were right too. Because what happened with Clive was such a shock to me. I know it's not the same thing at all as a loving relationship, or even what we did today, but...I probably wasn't ready yet no matter how much I thought otherwise."

"The part that haunts me, even now..." Dane pinched the bridge of his nose until Joy brushed his hand aside and kissed him affectionately, soothingly. When she stroked his hair, he admitted, "If I had done what Walker said and slept with you, I could have made it obvious around Wildfire. Where I went wrong was trying to keep things between us private and discreet because I thought I was looking out for you—"

"Oh." Joy's smile faded. "That's why you blame yourself?"

"There are a lot of things I'd change if I could. Yes. If we'd done things Walker's way, and everyone knew you were already mine, there wouldn't have been any claim for Clive to stake. Those guys are assholes, every one of them, but screwing with someone's old lady is one of the things they take dead serious." Dane drew several shallow breaths to keep a panic attack at bay. He hadn't had one of those in a few years, but when he had, Walker had been there to calm him down and distract him. He got himself together before continuing, "I'm not aggressive enough, never have been. And you're the one that paid the price for it. Walker's way better at that than me. When we're together, he takes care of it for us."

"You balance each other out." Joy folded her hands on his chest, then rested her chin on her fingers. "I always thought that about your friendship, so it makes sense that it's true in bed too."

"So what will I do without my other half? Will I still be a man you're interested in having as your partner without him? I can't even imagine it, Joy."

It struck him then that he might have redefined their boundaries again. It might already be too late to go back to what they had been. Hell, that might have changed the night they'd slept with Joy and got her pregnant, even if they hadn't realized it then.

"Don't freak out, Dane." Joy kissed his cheek. "Walker approves of this. Us."

"He says he does. But deep down..." Dane shook his head. "No, I don't think so. He's always desired you for himself. This peace won't last. It's going to break us all apart. And as much as I love you—and I swear to God I do, Joy—I don't know if I can live with wounding him like I've done to you. Worst of all, I'm tired of hurting myself. I don't want to lose either of you, as my friends or my lovers. That might be selfish as fuck but there it is. What the fuck are we going to do?"

"He's not going to be mad or hold it against us," Joy tried to reassure him with a soft laugh. "Hell, he's the one who sent me to you."

"What you do mean?" Dane sat up straight, dumping Joy onto the pillows as his eyes narrowed.

"The other day, he told me to seduce you because we were meant to be together."

"So that's why you did this?" Dane asked, horrified.

"Not because you wanted to sleep with me, but because Walker told you to? That's fucked up, Joy."

He rolled from bed and stood up, yanking on his pants. Now that his dick wasn't influencing his decisions, he thought he might have royally screwed up. Again.

"Dane…that's not exactly—"

"Fuck that. When is he going to learn he doesn't pull the strings? He's acting like his scumbag father, trying to rule everyone's lives and orchestrate what he thinks is best for them. I'm not a pawn in his dirty games, and you and Arden sure as hell shouldn't be either. I'm going to kick his motherfucking ass. Maybe it's time I grew some balls and did things the way I was expected to before, no matter how much I hated it."

"Dane, this is a mistake. Wait!"

"No, I'm done waiting. I'm done being the nice guy. The doormat. Fuck this." Dane stomped to the door, jammed his boots on his feet, then cracked his knuckles. He was going to fix this shit once and for all.

16

Walker swung the mallet one last time to finish rough-shaping a fender. He set the tool on the floor. Dripping with sweat from his workout, which had also served to vent some of his physical frustration, he headed over to his bench, where he planned to put the metal down too. *Planned to* because he never got that far. The clomp of booted feet came up behind him, triggering his instincts. He turned toward the person rapidly approaching. And that's when Dane's fist collided with his eye socket.

"What the fuck!" Walker roared as he dropped the chunk of metal with a clang loud enough to wake all the babies in Middletown, Arden and Noah included.

Habit had his fists balled and raised, his stance widened and his focus lasered in on his best friend in time to block the second swing that came his way. Dane's fist glanced off his forearm as he protected his head. It had been a while since they'd gone at it like this.

Walker didn't appreciate the reminder of their old life and their old ways. Weren't they better than this shit now?

"You tried to foist her off on me like you're some kind of noble pimp?" Dane lunged, reminding Walker of how fast and agile he was. He landed another blow, this time to Walker's gut.

Walker didn't enjoy the thought of hitting other guy, but he wasn't a punching bag either.

It wouldn't be the first time they'd scrapped in their nearly twenty-year friendship. Nor would it likely be the last. At least that's what he thought until he saw the rage twisting Dane's usually affable face into something he didn't recognize.

Maybe this time he'd crossed a line. Dane was always more sensitive when Joy was involved. Had he done something to break them for good?

"Hey, calm down." He tried to hold Dane at arm's length while the guy attempted to pummel him. They grappled, Walker grunting when he caught Dane's elbow in his ribs. It didn't hurt nearly as much as the part of him that mourned the loss of Dane and Joy. This was only more proof that he needed to get out of their way and let them grow together. "I'm happy for you two. Honestly."

He was. But part of him twisted in agony. The part that was going to have to let go of Dane like he'd already let go of Joy.

Walker wasn't sure he would survive.

"You don't get it!" Dane boomed, and broke free of Walker's hold.

Next thing he knew the other guy had launched himself at Walker and they were both about to crash to the cement garage floor. Walker wrapped his arms around Dane and threw his weight to one side so he absorbed the brunt of the force. Plus Dane landed on top of him, knocking the wind from him.

That gave Dane the opportunity to crumple Walker's shirt in his fists and shake him several times, hard enough to rattle his teeth. "You don't have the right to play God. You're not my president. This isn't Wildfire and you're not your motherfucking father, so quit acting like him!"

That did it.

Walker went completely still, indignity sparking his own rage. Unlike Dane, however, he got quieter and more deadly when he was pissed.

"So you're telling me you didn't enjoy whatever it was you two were doing in there?" He shouldn't have goaded Dane when he was already so worked up. And yet...he couldn't help himself. "Sounded to me and the rest of Middletown like you were having one hell of a time. Joy too."

A slow, wide slash of a smile spread across his face. Mostly because he'd been picturing what had been going on in their tiny home and convincing himself that he shouldn't run back there to join in.

It was why he'd started banging on that piece of metal in the first place.

"If you don't want to be involved, don't you dare even think about Joy like that. You don't deserve her either." Did Dane say either because he still believed *he* didn't deserve Joy or because he thought Walker wasn't good enough for either Joy or Dane?

Both were probably true.

Distracted, Walker didn't dodge the next volley of blows. Stunned, he absorbed the full impact of Dane's aggravation.

"Dane! Stop it!" Joy came nearer, trying to rip him off Walker. And when it became apparent that he wasn't going to budge, she started shouting for backup. "Quinn! Trevon! Gavyn! Wren! Van! Ollie! Anybody!"

Both Walker and Dane ignored her and kept hashing things out their way.

"When are you going to admit it, Walker?" Dane had the upper hand. He was fully on top of Walker now, using his forearm on Walker's throat to keep him pinned down while he tried to force a response.

"Admit what?" Walker croaked. There were plenty of things he could go to confession for. Which one did Dane have in mind?

"That you want to nail your stepsister so bad it's been driving you crazy for years. That you're not going to be happy for your whole damn life because you refuse to accept the one thing that will fill the gaping hole in your soul. That I'm a poor substitute for what you've always really needed and never let yourself have, and now you're trying to get rid of me while you can do it with a clear conscience."

That was it. Walker used his bulk and his fury to flip Dane, splaying him out on the concrete floor as Joy shrieked at them in the background. Even still he didn't plan on hitting the other guy. That wasn't his style anymore. Instead they wrestled, reminding him of the nights they'd done something similar in bed. Except this time it was all pain and no pleasure as Dane's knee connected with his balls.

"Hey, hey!" Trevon reached them first, sticking his arm between him and Dane. The guy risked getting it broken right off.

"That's enough!" Quinn bellowed, making Walker pause. He looked up, and that's when Dane clocked him again on his chin. "Dane! Quit it. This isn't Wildfire. We don't settle shit like this around here. You're going to have to use your fucking words instead of your fists. Settle down."

By the time Walker's vision returned to normal, Van had grabbed Dane's arms and pinned them behind him. He lifted Dane off Walker with a shocking ease that made it clear he had some experience in manhandling assailants. Walker knew the other guy was a beast and head of Kason's security, but he felt even more comfortable having Joy and Arden at Hot Rides with people like him around.

He collapsed to the garage floor, trying to catch his breath.

"Are you okay?" Joy rushed to his side and dabbed at his lip with the hem of her shirt. Dane's knuckle must have split it open.

Great, now he looked like a pussy on top of refusing to fight back. "Fine."

Despite what Dane had accused, he wasn't his father. He wasn't planning on being anything like that bastard when he grew up. So maybe he needed to take Dane's accusations to heart. It wasn't only the simple things like obeying the law that would differentiate him.

Shit.

Still, he let Quinn help him to his feet as Trevon and Gavyn positioned themselves between him and Dane to prevent them from clashing again. After a few seconds, Dane quit struggling against Van's iron grip. His brain reengaged.

"Shit. Sorry. I'm good now. You can let me go." Dane dropped his head, staring at the floor. Walker had preferred it when he was full of aggression rather than deflated.

"You're not going to start anything with him, are you?" Gavyn asked as he eyed Walker.

"What I'm going to do is keep minding my fucking business and get back to work." Walker used his wrist to swipe at the blood trickling from his lip.

"Nah, you're done for the day." Gavyn put one hand on his shoulder to soften his decree, then shoved gently in the direction of their cabin. "You three have serious stuff to figure out. And I don't want to see you back in the shop until you do. Arden and Noah are in the office. A lot of us came from rough places. That's not the kind of environment we want for our kids. This can't happen again—not at Hot Rides and not anywhere if you're really trying to start fresh—hear me?"

"Damn it. I fucked up...more." Dane slammed his eyes shut. He wasn't entirely to blame, though. They all knew it.

Walked cursed under his breath since it had been his fault. Dane had a long fuse and he'd still managed to set the guy off. "You're absolutely right. I might have screwed up again but that's exactly what I've been trying to avoid, dragging Arden into my old world, my old ways."

"How's that working out for you?" Quinn asked him with a raised brow. "Try a different approach, Walker."

As if he'd been talking to Joy instead, she nodded, then took one of Walker's hands in hers. Their connection erased each one of his aches in an instant.

"Gavyn, can you keep watching Arden for a few hours?" she asked.

"Yeah, of course." He grinned. "And next time I want to be alone with Amber, you'll get us back, right?"

"Absolutely." Then she reached out and held her other hand toward Dane. "Let's go home."

Dane stared at her for a few seconds too long, so Van bumped Dane's shoulder blade with the base of his palm. "Don't you be stupid, too. You're right to fight. There's better ways to do it than this, though."

"I apologize, Gavyn," Dane said before turning to Quinn asking forgiveness from him too. "I'll do better. *Be* better. I just..."

"We've all been there." Trevon grinned at Quinn. "Sometimes you wish you could strangle the people you love most."

Quinn shot his husband Trevon the finger, but they both laughed.

"Truth is, it wouldn't help if you did." Ollie chimed in. His words had a visible impact on Dane, since the two of them had struck up a pretty solid friendship. They were alike in a lot of ways, this one included.

"Yeah, I'm figuring that out." Dane looked like he hated himself right then.

And that did nothing to improve Walker's mood. Doing nothing, staying out of Joy and Dane's way, conspiring to bring them together... None of those things had made them any happier or more whole at the end of the day.

As Joy tugged Walker and Dane toward their tiny home, Quinn called, "Don't come back until you've kissed and made up!"

Wren, who'd emerged from her welding booth at the tail end of the ruckus, snapped a rag in Quinn's direction, but when Walker glanced over his shoulder, they were talking together in hushed, concerned tones as they stood in a line and watched him, Dane, and Joy go.

He wondered if it had been this hard for them to work

out their unconventional relationships. He'd have to ask to hear their stories sometime.

But not today. Because he had more important shit to figure out first.

Was Quinn right? Did he need to try a different approach?

Was Dane right? Had he been pulling the same shit his father did to try to control everyone around him?

Was Gavyn right? Was he setting Arden up to struggle like they had in a household rife with contention and chaos?

That wasn't his goal. None of it.

They piled inside their house and stood facing each other in a rough triangle that occupied the center of their living area. Dane's chest still heaved as a result of his exertion and the emotional outpouring that had fueled it. Joy glared at them both.

Walker swallowed hard and prepared to man up. Even if that meant something completely different from what he'd always assumed. "I think I made a mistake."

"You *think*?" Joy crossed her arms. The motion highlighted her chest, which threatened to spill over the top of the tank top she'd obviously thrown on without a bra before chasing after Dane.

"Okay, I get it." Walker held his hands up. "I know I screwed this up. I'm sorry."

Dane looked up then with wide eyes.

"Is it so unbelievable that I would fucking apologize?"

"Yes," he and Joy said in unison.

And then she continued, "Are you saying sorry that it came to this or are you remorseful because you've realized that we love you and you plan to do something positive about it? Like cracking open your big, stupid heart, and letting us both in once and for all?"

"I don't know." Did she have to jump right in with difficult questions? "It's hard for me to see how getting tangled up between you two is going to fix anything. I'm detrimental to your future, and Arden's. With me around, you'll never fully be free of Angus. We'll always have to be looking over our shoulders. It's never going to end. You heard Gavyn. We have to break the cycle, if not for ourselves, then for Arden's sake."

"If we stand and fight together, I think we're strong enough to make it." Joy squeezed his hand, and probably Dane's too. "Especially with the support of the Hot Rides gang and their friends. They're everything Wildfire never was."

"I'm prepared for the possibility that one of us, or all of us, could get hurt. It's worth the risk." Dane looked grim as fuck as he said it, his voice shredded.

"I'm tired of running," Joy said, nodding. "What's the point of struggling so long if I don't get to live my life the way I want?"

Walker looked back and forth between them trying to figure out another reason he couldn't accept what they were offering. "Are you sure, Joy? We're not easy men, either of us, and both together...we're a lot."

Dane didn't argue with that. In fact, he piled on. "Plus, you know there's something between us too. Is that what you have in mind for yourself? To be caught up in our freak show?"

"Whose fucking side are you on?" Joy wrenched her hand from Dane's and glared at him.

Uh oh.

"I'm being realistic. These are all things we need to

consider. I have no doubt that sex between the three of us would be phenomenal. The night we spent together was incredible." Dane adjusted his junk as if he hadn't spent the better part of the last three hours making Joy scream.

"I thought that's what you wanted, too. To be whole." Joy flinched as if Dane had shoved her away. "Isn't that why you went after Walker?"

"No. I did that because he keeps trying to make decisions for us, which is bullshit."

"And how is what you're doing right now, to me, any different?" Joy accused.

Walker figured she was right on that point, but he didn't mind Dane doing whatever it took to protect her, even if it was from themselves.

Dane sputtered. "Because you've never seen us together. You don't know what you're asking for."

"Right. So, let's put it to a test. Why don't the two of you kiss and make up, like Quinn said, but let me watch. And we'll see exactly what my reaction is so no one has to jump to any conclusions for anyone else." She grinned slowly and surely. "I'm pretty sure I know the answer already, but fair enough. Let's prove me right."

Walker and Dane squared off and met each other's stares. Equal parts questioning and hungry. After their tussle, Walker felt compelled to show Dane that he wasn't holding any grudges and to reassure him that, no matter what happened, they were going to be okay. They'd always managed to come through things before. At least when they stuck together.

"I forgive you for decking me." Walker stepped closer. He put his hand up, cupping the spot on Dane's cheek that already showed hints of a faint purple stain. If he gave Joy what she wanted, maybe that would solve their problems. It might disgust her or push her away. Then they wouldn't have to fight anymore.

He was selfish enough to admit there was some appeal to that scenario.

Walker wasn't sure he could give Dane up, even if he should. Today had proved that to him. He'd been scared shitless as he worked in the garage that his plan might have worked a little too well and he'd be left with no one.

Try something different, Quinn had said.

Well, here went nothing.

17

Joy held her breath as Walker leaned in and very softly brushed his lips against Dane's. It wasn't anything like she'd been expecting. He didn't smash their mouths together and ravish his best friend, though she suspected that's how they came together most times.

It might have been because of his split lip, but honestly she thought it was actually because of their wounded egos and the damage they'd done to each other's insides. As much as she'd hated watching them fight, she adored seeing them build each other back up.

Dane moaned, then put his hands on Walker's shoulders. He parted them just far enough and long enough to whisper, "That will never happen again. I really am sorry."

"No need," Walker answered before putting his arms around Dane and holding him close for a few seconds before he sealed their mouths more completely the second time.

What started as a gentle homecoming didn't stay that way for long.

Surprisingly, it was Dane who blinked first, grabbing the back of Walker's shirt in his hands as if he was afraid the other man might fly away or vanish from beneath his touch. How could Walker not realize that cutting himself out of the picture also meant tearing himself out of Dane's soul?

Dane would never recover from a loss like that. Joy knew it and accepted it. She acknowledged them and whatever it was they had grown into. She had no intentions of giving Walker the boot so that she and Dane could enjoy some sort of selfish, isolated relationship. After all, she planned to be less like her own mother, who'd always taken the easy way out and favored convenience over true emotions in her marriage.

Walker should understand that considering he fought so hard to be nothing like Angus.

Even more important, seeing them still together after all this time, terrified of losing each other, proved to her they were capable of commitment and loyalty to their partner. It eased the part of her that still worried they would abandon her again.

They had it in them to go the distance with each other and...hopefully...with her.

So she was willing to give them everything she had in the hopes that she could claim even some of them in return. It would be more than enough to fill her heart.

The guys inched closer to each other until they were standing chest to chest and dick to dick. Their hands and arms roamed across each other's backs and shoulders. Joy didn't dare blink, so she saw the effect it had on Dane when Walker grabbed his ass and used the hold to press them more tightly together.

If she was the type of woman to be triggered easily, she might not have been able to handle seeing them so into each other that they appeared to forget she was even standing there, mere inches from them. At least until Walker cast his gaze to the side and caught her ogling them like some extra invasive Peeping Tom.

He cast his attention back to Dane and practically hummed, "She likes it, Dane. She's into this. Us. And what we can do to each other."

Dane made a low sound in his throat and shivered, pouring himself into the kiss as frantically as he'd thrown himself at Walker in the garage minutes earlier.

If they didn't love each other intensely, there wouldn't be any way they could get so upset at each other. If they didn't care, it would be easy to say fuck it and walk away. They couldn't and neither could she allow it.

No matter what else happened, Joy could never live with herself if she was the reason they lost each other. No way.

If she was the wedge driving them apart, she'd pack up and leave.

Except, wasn't that exactly what Walker had tried to do to preserve her relationship with Dane? Shit, yes. The only solution was to stand and fight. For each other.

And that's what she planned to do.

As soon as the guys finished apologizing to each other by way of a lot of tongue and grinding action. *Damn*.

Joy squeezed her thighs together, trying to soothe the ache developing between them as she watched Walker and Dane make out. They were so damn handsome, masculine, and still exposed. Open to emotion, unlike so many of the guys she'd spent her formative years around at Wildfire.

Nothing could have been more appealing to her.

She took a tiny step closer, tempted to put her hands on them and join in their exchange. If they didn't do something about the molten desire bubbling up within her, more furiously by the second, she was going to erupt. Did they even realize how fucking hot they were making her?

And when they broke apart, she could see the passion shining from their eyes equally as brightly as it must be from her own. They turned to her as if they were one person.

Walker said, "So? What do you think?"

"I think I need you to take me to bed," Joy demanded. "Both of you."

"Joy, we just…" Dane flicked his gaze toward the room they'd shared earlier. She was well aware of what they'd done there, and she couldn't wait to do it again. He certainly wasn't having any issues getting revved up again either. "You should probably take a long bath and let me give you a massage instead."

Walker took one look at her face and said, "Now you did it."

And that was even before she propped her hands on her hips and drew a deep breath to roast Dane's ass. Although he'd held his own earlier, Walker stepped in to protect his best friend, as always.

"Maybe he's right. We should use tonight to think things over." He tried to appear reasonable. Or was he trying to buy them some time to avoid committing to the very thing he'd been trying to resist.

Now both Joy and Dane bristled.

Joy Ride

Dane growled, "You're backing out already? I don't have to reexamine the situation. I'm only worried about Joy since we fucked like rabbits this afternoon."

"Well, don't. I'm fine. And I've thought this over. And over and over. For years before and extra this past one," Joy practically snarled. "If you're still not sure this is for you, say that. But don't act like I might not know what I want."

"I didn't mean it like that..." Except it sure sounded like he had.

"This isn't Wildfire. I'm not your old lady or some shit." Joy stood taller, prepared to fight as ferociously as Dane had if necessary to finish hammering some sense into Walker. Dane, too, for that matter. "If I can make my own decisions and I'm an equal like you two keep insisting I am, then let me choose this. Because I want you both."

"You're right. I shouldn't have tried to dissuade you. You know your own body and your own heart. If this is what you're after, I'm in." Dane stepped closer to her and wrapped an arm around her waist, tugging her against his side in a show of unity. At least she could count on him again.

"And you, Walker?" Joy leveled her best mom glare at him.

He didn't budge.

So she gave in a little...okay, a lot...and begged, "Please?"

"Fuck." He slammed his eyes shut and drew in several ragged breaths. "It's always been nearly impossible to stay away from you. Obviously, since we couldn't resist temptation that night before we left Wildfire. But seeing you and Dane, side by side, offering yourselves up. Son of a bitch. I don't stand a chance, do I?"

"No." Dane grinned. "You can regret it in the morning."

Joy hoped that if he fell off the no-threesomes wagon now, he was going to binge on them the entire night in case it was the last time she got to experience the rush of having the only two men she would ever love lavish their attention on her.

Hell, she'd thought they'd already had their one and only shot so she'd cherished every moment, reliving it in her dreams often.

"Fine." Walker crossed his arms. "I still believe you would be better off without me or the complications Angus will bring to us, even if he's been acting chill for now. He's still out there, waiting for the right opportunity to fuck with me. A threat to you both and Arden."

"We have better odds sticking together." Dane hugged Joy as if to promise he wasn't going to let go.

Walker dropped his head back, stared at the ceiling, and blew out a breath. "This is a terrible idea, but you're both adults and you're welcome to make bad decisions."

"You could never be the wrong choice for me," Joy told Walker. The fact that he gave a shit about what was best for her and their daughter told her everything she needed to know. "You either, Dane."

Walker took a step forward and then another until he was crowding them both where they were still linked, embracing as they met their future head on.

"Kiss," he commanded. "Let me see how you are together."

Was he asking because it turned him on to see two people he was attracted to pleasing each other, or because

Joy Ride

he needed the reminder to help him stay on course and distance himself from them so that he could flee later, when his better sense kicked in?

Joy wasn't sure, but the only hope she had was to take a chance and risk everything.

Maybe no matter what Walker's intentions were now, if they did this, it would cement their bond. As enjoyable as sex with Dane had been earlier, it wasn't...this. This all-consuming compulsion to fling herself into the tempest of emotions they kicked up when they were near her, together.

"You heard the man," Dane said quietly as he turned toward her and used his knuckle beneath her chin to tip her face toward his. "Why don't we show him what he missed out on when he was being a dumbass?"

Joy grinned and nodded before putting her hand on the back of Dane's head and bringing him close enough that she could see the flecks of gold in his irises. He was like a bobcat. At a glance he might look docile, or even tamed, but there was a beast inside and she couldn't wait to unleash it.

Apparently Walker was right there with her. He prodded Dane. "You're going to let her do the work? Show her how badly you've needed her for all these years. Joy's right there in your arms, Dane. You have her. What are you going to do with her now?"

Joy felt the vibration of Dane's chest as a strangled roar left his throat. She didn't have much time to analyze it, though, since his mouth landed on hers a moment later.

She tried to soothe him with repeated strokes of her fingers against his scalp, but it was no use.

So instead she simply hung on and absorbed the flood

of his desire, longing, and a whole lot of tongue action. She didn't even feel bad when his thigh slid between hers and she began to ride it, using him to alleviate the ache in her core.

She had no idea how long they kissed, but it was enough to make her aware of the changes to her body that he'd already inspired. Her nipples were hard, her face felt hot, and her muscles were loose and heavy. A little bit more and she'd be in danger of coming before they'd even made it to the bedroom. She couldn't help if it his leg fit perfectly between hers, giving her clit something to rub on while they made out.

"That's so sexy," Walker hummed before he pried them apart. "Now I want to see you do it naked."

18

At least they could save a step since Dane had never gotten around to putting his shirt on before storming out to the garage. His lean build was impressive, powerful yet sleek.

He reached for his jeans.

"No." Walker swatted his hands away. "Let her."

He put his palm on Joy's lower back then, encouraging her to unwrap her prize.

Joy fumbled the button once, twice, as his hard-on made the fabric tighter than usual on his trim hips. When she finally popped it open, the zipper wedged shut. So she slid her hand inside to make sure she didn't injure Dane when she gave it a solid tug.

Of course, she also took the opportunity to cup his dick and squeeze it lovingly a few times while she was at it.

Walker chuckled when Dane groaned and breathed through his nose.

"See how much he wants you, Joy?" Walker murmured in her ear from entirely too close behind her to encourage her brain to function properly. "He always has. You've always been his dream girl."

"Woman," she corrected.

"Now you are," Walker acceded. "To us both. Keep going. Get those jeans off him."

Walker might not be anything like his father, but he had inherited some of his ringleader tendencies. Joy was more than happy to let him exercise them here, in private. They came in handy when both she and Dane were mindless with desire and eager to submit to Walker's alpha nature, which would guarantee the potential ecstasy they could bring each other manifested itself.

The truth was, she and Dane had floundered on their own, neither one willing to make the first move even when they'd so badly craved action. Walker was the catalyst that took their potential and sparked it. Without him, there was only a lot of latent desire and no active reaction.

"Stop thinking and do it, Joy," Walker growled at her, slapping her ass. Then he hesitated. "Unless you've changed your mind."

She blinked, then grabbed the waistband of Dane's jeans and yanked them to the floor. He helped her finish the job by kicking them off. Then he stood there, completely nude and unashamed, his cock hard and ready for whatever games Walker would play with them.

"Now you, Dane. Show me how beautiful she is."

"Like you forgot," Dane huffed, and rolled his eyes. "It's only been a few days since you buried your mouth in her sweet pussy and made her come all over your face, hasn't it?"

For a second, Walker looked like he might get pissed, or end their session right then.

Then he sighed and said, "Yes. Sorry. I should have told you about that."

"I only wish I'd been there to see it for myself." Dane was cute when he pouted.

"How about I give you a repeat performance?" Walker offered and Joy's legs wobbled. She certainly wasn't going to dissuade him if he wanted to let her have a do over.

"I'll take it." Dane grinned.

"Then you'd better get her clothes off, huh?" Walker grabbed Dane's dick and led him closer to Joy. "Go ahead. I'm patient, but I can't wait forever."

Dane might have followed orders, but he did it with his own twist. After ridding her of her tank top, he kept her back to Walker so he couldn't become distracted by her boobs. Then he slid her sweats down so the waistband perched barely below her ass cheeks before encouraging her to lean on his shoulders so she was bent forward. He stroked her flank, clearly trying to get Walker back for making them tease each other so mercilessly.

She wanted to rip her clothes off, and instead they were making her crazy doing it bit by bit.

"You have the finest ass I've ever seen," Walker groaned, and stepped closer. He rubbed his jeans-covered hard-on along the crack of it, making her shiver. "I can't wait until the day I fuck it."

"Why not today?" she asked with a glance over her shoulder.

"Because I have other things in mind." Walker spanked her once, sharp though not very hard. He stepped back and barked at Dane, "Keep going."

At least he was planning on fucking her again in the future. For now, Joy would settle for that newsflash.

Dane didn't torture them much more. He made quick

work of her sweats, helping her step out of them. She leaned on his broad shoulders, never once fearing she might tip over when she had someone as steady as him to lean on.

Then he stood, so she did too, both of them naked and neither embarrassed to put themselves on display for Walker's approval.

"Now we're getting somewhere." He paced a circle around them, admiring their nude forms from every angle. He dragged his fingertips over Joy's breasts and lingered on her ass before caressing Dane's shoulders and staring pointedly at his cock. "I see you've recovered from this afternoon as well."

"Ten years of longing can't be erased by a single afternoon of sex. Even if it is *spectacular* sex." Dane beamed as he met Joy's stare.

"Well, then why don't you two get over here and strip me so I can do something about that?"

Joy didn't have to be told twice. She rushed to Walker and immediately slid her hands beneath his shirt, as she'd wanted to do since the first time she'd first seen him slaving away at Hot Rides without one.

Damn, he'd grown up fine. His muscles drew her fingers like magnets.

Having the liberty to explore each ridge and valley of his physique was a freedom she had craved for as long as she could remember. The glimpse she'd gotten beneath his wet T-shirt the other day in the bathroom hadn't helped her obsession any. Unlike Dane, he was bulky and a little coarse. He had more chest hair and of course those gorgeous tattoos that spanned his chest.

She couldn't wait to lick the outline of each one.

While she edged his shirt up, exposing his abs and

then his pecs, Dane got to work on Walker's pants. If they teamed up, they could get to the good stuff twice as fast. That didn't mean she didn't pause to take a peek when Dane revealed Walker's cock and set it free from the confines of his soft, work-worn jeans.

The rips in the knees and thighs were sexy but didn't look half as good as him without them on at all. His thighs were bunched and powerful, exactly like the rest of him.

Walker lifted his arms, snapping her back to her task. She licked her lips as she drew the soft cotton over his head, then waited while he threaded his arms through it before she tossed it into the corner, forgotten.

It wouldn't bother her if he never put another one on.

Damn, he was sexy.

When he grinned at her and Dane, she realized they were both gawking at him. How could they not when he stood there wearing only his beard, and his cock promised that he really was as attracted to them as they were to him?

"Since you both seem to be fascinated by my dick, why don't you take a closer look? On your knees. Now." Walker pressed Dane's shoulder, urging him to kneel.

He did, taking Joy's hand in his and tugging her so she joined him at Walker's feet.

She didn't mind, considering Walker had done the same for her recently.

Hell, she'd practically begged to return the favor then. It felt only fair to do so now.

He put a hand on each of their heads and rubbed his thumbs over their temples. The soft caress made his direct words feel inspiring instead of confrontational.

"You're drooling, Dane." Walker's smirk made Joy

either want to smack him or fuck his brains out. She wasn't sure which.

Okay, yes, she knew exactly which.

Dane scrubbed his mouth with his forearm, though he never took his gaze from Walker's crotch.

"So are you." Dane said with a grin. They stared, transfixed, as a bead of precome rolled down the head of Walker's cock and dripped, like a liquid pearl, to the floor.

"Who's going to suck me first?" Walker asked them.

"Me." Dane turned to Joy. "Is that okay with you?"

She nodded since she figured this might also be his way of making up for trying to dent Walker's handsome face. "I can't wait to see you go down on him. I bet he loves it when you do."

Walker groaned and tightened his grip on them, tangling his fingers in their hair.

Next thing she knew, he was massaging her scalp, making her want to rub up against his leg like a kitten. Joy acted on instinct, reaching out to stroke his cock, which was already rock hard. It only took a few pumps of her hand from his tip to the base before it felt like he would overflow her grasp.

Dane surprised her when he put his hand over hers and tightened his grip, forcing her to apply more pressure. "He likes it harder than that. Hold him like this."

It made her wet to think of how Dane knew that and the extensive experience they obviously had pleasing each other. She wasn't jealous of their affair, but she did regret that she hadn't been there to see them make love to each other. She bet it was amazing to watch.

Maybe soon they would put on a show for her.

Or, better yet, let her be involved, like this.

Dane used her hand to jerk Walker's cock. And when

he'd set the pace, he left her to do it on her own while he moved on to other areas so they could wage a multi-pronged attack on Walker's restraint.

Dane removed his hand and replaced it with his mouth, first sipping the fluid from the tip of Walker's dick like it was a delicacy before dropping lower to nuzzle Walker's heavy balls.

"Yes. Lick them while she jacks my cock." Walker gasped when Dane did as instructed, taking as much of Walker's sac into his mouth as possible. His neck strained as he lapped at the sensitive skin before pulling on it with light draws of his lips.

Joy figured she could do one better.

She slid her fist to the base of Walker's shaft, the side of her hand tapping Dane's lips. He kissed her there while tending to Walker too. Several inches of Walker's cock jutted from the ring of her fingers, so she dipped down to engulf them in her mouth. At the last second, she whispered to Dane, "Do you mind?"

The motion he created when he shook his head no must have felt amazing.

Walker cursed. He tightened his grip on them involuntarily as his hands flexed in response to the sensations they bombarded him with.

So she piled on more by engulfing his shaft in the wet warmth of her mouth. Together, they serviced him, reveling in each groan and curse that slipped from his lips while they spoiled him.

When Joy retreated, needing to give her jaw a rest, Dane was right there. He aimed Walker's dick toward himself, then took the entire thing into his throat, whereas she would have choked. He bobbed over Walker, moaning as he filled his mouth with the other man's thick cock.

Joy didn't have a lot of experience, but she had the internet. Both Dane and Walker were impressive compared to the movies she'd watched while imagining them in the performers' places.

After only a few minutes of Dane's unrestrained oral treatment, Walker shouted, "Enough!"

Dane blinked as he let Walker's hard-on go with a wet pop. "I was just getting started," he said with a wink at Joy, who laughed.

Sex with Dane was fun. But this...this was getting serious.

"I have to fuck." Walker reached down and grabbed Joy beneath her arms. He used his hold to pluck her from the floor and lift her. Except he didn't make it as far as his bedroom, despite the short distance to their ultimate destination.

Instead, he handed her to Dane. She wasn't sure exactly what they were doing, but they apparently could communicate telepathically, or they were riding the same dirty wavelength or something, because she ended up with the back of one shoulder resting on the top of Dane's, where he braced her as if it was the most natural thing in the world instead of a gymnastic maneuver.

He still knelt on the ground. So when Walker grabbed her hips and held them at waist height, she found herself suspended like bridge between them.

"Keep her there," he directed Dane. "Right there. That's perfect."

Joy did what she could to stabilize herself, which meant wrapping her legs around Walker's hips, her heels crossing in the small of his back. One of her arms went around Dane's back, her hand curling beneath his arm, around his ribs.

Joy Ride

The position left his hand on that side free to roam across her body. Of course, he went straight for her breasts. Even back in high school his eyes had always been drawn to her cleavage. Now, even more so.

"Don't worry, we've got you," Walker promised with a toothy smile that made him seem more like the Big Bad Wolf than a prince. She definitely approved.

Dane squeezed her breast lightly, with the technique he'd developed during their earlier interlude. He brushed his thumb over her nipple with a feather-light pressure that made her squirm against Walker.

"You need me too, don't you?" Walker asked her. How could he doubt it?

"Yes. Fuck me." She couldn't bear for there to be any doubt.

Last time they'd been together, they'd used condoms, though clearly they weren't flawless. This time, Joy wasn't about to pause to see if Dane or Walker had any handy. Walker, however, stopped just before his cock could burrow inside her and replace the ache they'd inspired with relief.

"What about protection?" he asked her.

"I'm good with this if you are. I was tested during my pregnancy. There's no reason why we can't go for it like this." She would have shrugged if she could. It was probably irresponsible to chance having another baby, but she loved their daughter so much she would be thrilled to have another now that she would be able to provide for them. "Besides, Dane and I didn't use anything earlier."

"Son of a bitch!" Even then, Dane didn't wobble, he held her steady as he stammered. "I wasn't thinking."

"You fucked her bare?" Walker's eyes widened and his

pupils dilated, though more due to envy than ire it seemed. His nostrils flared and his cock jerked between her legs.

Joy squirmed, trying to align them better. It was impossible without reaching for him. She could have done that with her free hand, but something in her told her he wanted to do the honors. So she tried to be patient, and wait.

"Yes. Fuck yes." Dane kissed her cheek. "And I don't regret a single moment. It was the best sex of my life. And I can't wait to do it again. A million times."

Walker grunted as if Dane had gotten in another punch to the gut. "I bet."

"Best sex of my life *with a woman*. How about that?" Dane chuckled and Walker grumbled.

"I'll have to step up my game with you. Later." Walker shot Dane a look that meant he was in some serious trouble, if by trouble you meant a world-class orgasm or twenty.

Joy hoped they'd let her watch.

Her pussy clenched at the thought.

Walker was there, dipping a finger into her, giving her something to hug as her body tried to grant itself some relief. "You like the thought of that, huh?"

"Yeah." She panted. "But not right now. Right now I need you. Inside me. Please."

Walker smiled down at her. "Since you asked so prettily. Of course."

The first nudge of his head at her opening nearly made her scream his name. It had been so long since she'd felt the anticipation of him hovering there and even longer that she'd wanted to before that. If it wasn't for

Arden, she might have thought the one night they'd shared had been another dream.

But this...this was very, very real.

The increasing pressure of his tip penetrating her as he and Dane caught her between them made her wild. She arched, though the motion dislodged him.

So he took his cock in hand and fed it to her. He had more girth than Dane, though he wasn't quite as long. After everything they'd done earlier, she winced slightly as he spread her open, loosening the rings of muscle at her entrance so he could plunge deeper into her channel.

Where Dane was finesse and grace, Walker was pure power. He didn't hesitate or hedge. Instead, he sheathed himself with her body in a single fluid stroke that made his presence intimately known to her body. There was no denying he possessed her completely when his torso tapped her clit and her ass rested against his upper thighs.

Breath rushed out of her in a whoosh.

Thankfully, Dane was there. He truly had her, and she didn't only mean supporting her body. He murmured in her ear. "Relax, Joy. Let him in. Let him make you feel good. He's going to do such a good job fucking you."

"So did you," she said, staring into his eyes so he could see that it was true.

"Ah, but not like him." He kissed the corner of her mouth, which was the best he could do in their positions.

"If you two are able to have a whole conversation about me, then I'm not doing this right." Walker adjusted his hands so that he was essentially gripping Joy by the ass, his thumbs resting on her hipbones. His fingers squeezed and kneaded as he began to work within her. "Hold on, Joy."

19

Joy tightened her legs around Walker, increasing the clasp she had on Dane as well.

Good thing, too, because Walker wasn't kidding around. He anchored her as he began to thrust, first with short though sharp jabs that gradually magnified into full-length strokes. Several times, the fat head of his cock nearly slipped from her pussy. The reintroduction of his crown past her pubic bone made her shout and curse.

Not because she wanted him to stop—no, never—but because she wanted to experience that rush of rapture a million more times before she died.

Joy didn't do it on purpose, but her fingers curled, digging her nails into Dane's side. He hissed, then shuddered beneath her.

"Sorry," she said, or tried to—it came out as a croak, her throat drawn as tight as the rest of her.

"Don't be." Walker hammered into her a few more times, rocking her into Dane. "He likes it. At least as much as you do."

Could that be? Joy turned her head and raked her teeth over Dane's neck.

Sure enough, he groaned, and not in pain.

As if Dane's rapture amplified her own, her pussy squeezed Walker's cock. The three of them affected each other, even when they weren't directly touching. Walker and Dane were toying with each other through her, and she loved being the tool that brought them both pleasure.

"That's right." Walker's next thrust was harder. Deeper. "You're perfect for each other. You get each other off without even realizing it. You should see him staring at your tits right now. Should I make them bounce more for him?"

Joy couldn't believe Walker was talking to her like this, treating her as though she was a woman who could easily satisfy them both, handle their wicked desires, and not like a delicate girl who needed to be protected, especially from themselves and their intense needs.

It was heady, and for the first time, she felt powerful. In control of her life. Fully.

She also felt like she was going to shatter around Walker any second.

"Yeah, I think I should too." Walker tightened his hold, making her acutely aware of each of his fingertips. She might have bruises the next day, but she would wear them proudly.

He fucked into her with unrelenting speed and passion, proving to her that she'd never truly been claimed like this before. Hopefully this time he planned to keep her and to give her all of him in return. The collision of their bodies caused her breasts to rock, and even that motion added to her bliss.

But when Dane raised his free arm and laid his palm

low on her belly, she knew her time was running short. If he touched her clit right then, she was going to fly.

He didn't move to do it. Not until Walker gave him the green light.

"Going to shoot so hard in you when you come. Go ahead, Dane. Make her explode on my dick." Walker grunted. "I'm ready."

That made one of them. Joy wasn't prepared. Considering how long she'd waited for this moment, she wanted it to last so much longer. The reality was that neither of them had that kind of superhuman willpower. It was too good to resist.

So they'd simply have to do it again sometime. Hopefully sometime very soon. Like immediately after they finished doing it this time. It might make her greedy, but she'd held out so long, trusted only them to share such an intimate experience with her, that she hoped it never ended.

Joy had a lot of time to make up for.

When Walker dug in and began to pound inside her, she realized what she'd thought was an animalistic claiming was actually tame in comparison to him acting without restraint, as he was now. Rather than scare her, or harm her, his abandon made her proud. He believed she could handle it.

And she could.

No, more than that, she loved it.

Joy threw her head back on Dane's shoulder. She would have crashed to the floor then if they hadn't been fully supporting her weight, because every muscle in her body had one purpose and one only. To absorb the ecstasy Walker brought her with every thrust, groan, curse, and pump of his hips.

She clung to his dick, her pussy trying to keep him buried deep as he massaged her with his shuttling cock. And when the head locked against the tight ring at her entrance, they both shouted.

The next time he plunged into her, balls-deep, she surrendered.

Joy felt like she was unraveling from the center outward. Her orgasm ripped through her like a sonic boom, lighting up every nerve ending she possessed.

"Yes. Fuck, yes," Walker barked. "Me too."

She looked up in time to see his jaw set and the tendons in his neck standing out. Their contours lent to his primal image and were so damn attractive it magnified the effect he was having on her. She clenched around him, smothering him, hoping he knew that he was the only person in the world who could do this to her.

Well, him and Dane together. They touched her in different ways.

Tamed different parts of her being.

As she orgasmed, Walker did also. His abs rippled as his balls emptied inside her. He called her name with every pulse that filled her.

"That's so fucking hot," Dane murmured reverently. "You two are the most beautiful people I have ever seen. Thank you for letting me be here with you. For making me part of this."

Joy was too busy melting to answer him with words, but she hoped the blissful smile she shot him and the euphoria pouring from her gaze said enough.

Her legs went limp, dangling behind Walker as he slowed and gradually halted, only rocking into her every few seconds, when a lingering aftershock hit him. Each tiny movement made her spasm, completely in tune with his body.

Only when they'd both gone still did she realize what an awkward position she was in.

Walker pulled out, making her whimper. Without him, she felt so...empty.

He lowered her hips to the ground. Dane shifted from kneeling to sitting, then gathered her into his lap. She let her head rest on his chest as she caught her breath. He rocked her, combing her hair gently with his fingers while telling her how amazing she'd done and how special she was.

In the meantime, Walker used his discarded T-shirt to dry off his dick, then stood with his hands on his knees as if he'd run the couple miles to the Hot Rods garage and back as he sometimes did in the mornings.

"I wasn't done with that." She tried not to pout.

He laughed, then lifted his head to meet her dazed stare. "I'm good, but I'm only human. It needs a break."

"As long as it's not permanently broken." She smiled, unable to believe she was teasing him about something so sensual and he was grinning back, not calling what they'd done together a mistake. In the past he would have denied that he lusted after her, or bolted as soon as his hormones stopped running the show.

This time was different. Finally.

"Don't worry, Dane can fix it." Walker flashed her a lopsided smile. It had been so long since she'd seen the jovial side of him, she'd nearly forgotten it existed. The young man he'd been was still in there somewhere, camouflaged by responsibility, remorse, and disappointments.

Joy made it her new mission to bring it out of him more and more.

Dane hugged her tight as if he too approved of the old Walker making an appearance.

"So...are you being serious?" Walker asked her when he could manage to stand upright again. "You want more? Even after what you and Dane did this afternoon and just now..."

Should she admit it or pretend it had only been a joke? Joy hesitated for a second too long.

Walker approached and crouched down in front of her and Dane. "That was in no way a criticism. I know it's not my usual MO, but I'm asking what you want instead of assuming. Trying something new, like Quinn recommended."

"Novel concept." Dane snorted. Though he sobered quickly and said, "I'm not saying you shouldn't, Joy, but you have to be sore. Think about that before you push yourself. We'll have plenty of other chances..."

But would they really? Life had a way of screwing them over. Why should this time turn out better? No, she didn't care to risk it. They were here, and she felt like a dieter at an all-you-can-eat buffet on cheat day.

"I might not be able to walk tomorrow, but it'll be worth it." Joy grinned. "The other Hot Rides ladies will understand and help me with Arden while you're at work. Pretty sure."

Dane shook his head. "You're probably right. Hell, if I know them, they'll throw us a Finally Got Laid party."

"As long as Devra makes the cake, I'm in." Walker shrugged.

"Hang on a second..." Joy was almost afraid to ask, but

it sounded like... "Do you mean to say you haven't slept with anyone since you've been at Hot Rides?"

"Oh." Dane looked at Walker, who shrugged. "Yeah. We kind of took a vow of celibacy after you. It didn't feel right anymore. What we had been doing."

"Or doing it with someone who wasn't you. It was never going to be the same, Joy. Never," Walker told her, and unlocked her heart from the cell she'd kept it in since that night Clive had attacked her and she stopped believing in fairytales.

Their candor made it easy for her to repay them in kind. "I guess that's why I never slept with anyone besides you two. And never want to again. But with you... Yeah, I want more. I want everything."

Walker nodded as if that decided it. As if she had absolute power and control in their relationship. "In that case, get your asses in the bedroom."

Dane didn't mess around. He stood, lifting Joy with him as he went. She clung to him, hugging him with her arms and legs. If she felt a few twinges in muscles that hadn't ever been used as well as they had that day, she declined to say so. Because the truth was, she might never get enough of them.

So she had to take what she could while they were offering.

Dane laid her onto the mattress with her ass resting on the edge and her legs bent over the side, her feet on the floor.

Walker reached down and flipped her around like she was one of the parts he shaped and molded from a sheet of raw material into a beautiful work of functioning art like her motorcycle. *Hers.* They were granting her freedom bit by bit. In exchange, all she had to do was believe in them.

Walker would make her into the woman who could satisfy him if only she let him. So she did. Joy followed his unspoken commands, going into the position he guided her into—laying on her back with her heels near each corner of the wide, soft bed. He tucked her hands beneath her head so she was splayed and on display for them.

Then he smacked Dane's ass. "Go ahead, get in there with her. You're going to have to do the honors while you help me get ready again. Are you up for the job?"

Dane grinned. "Hell yes. Been training for this moment all my life."

He climbed in bed with her, careful not to jostle her from where Walker had set her. His legs occupied the space between hers, and he used his knees to press her thighs apart until he could fit comfortably between them.

"Now, use your fingers and make sure she's ready for you. Go slow," Walker ordered.

Then he turned to Joy. "Your only responsibility is to tell me right away if something he's doing doesn't feel good. If you're too sore or too tired, you let me know and we'll find another way to satisfy you. Or put you to bed."

"I swear I will." Joy knew with them nothing could feel bad.

"Other than that, enjoy." Walker traced a line down the center of her nose. The affectionate gesture rocked her more than his lust-fueled fucking had. She expected that from Dane, but not Walker. Maybe she should.

She turned her face to press a kiss to his palm and hoped he realized that he deserved the same kind of attention from them.

That's when Dane's fingers began to slip inside her

and she lost track of thoughts more complicated than *Holy shit. That feels amazing.* She moaned as her body stirred, coming back to life.

"You're messing with me, aren't you?" Dane asked Walker. "You know she's fucking soaked and you wanted me to feel it for myself. Especially after you pumped that huge load in her."

Walker chuckled. "Maybe. Why don't you lick your fingers clean and show her how much you like the taste of us together?"

"Son of a bitch." Dane's eyelids grew heavy and he withdrew his hand, making her sigh and shift restlessly, eager for more. Then he put the two digits in his mouth and sucked them, his cheeks hollowing as he obeyed Walker's orders.

"More?" Walker teased.

"Hell yes," Dane affirmed.

"And you?" He raised his brows at Joy.

She nodded.

"Then go ahead, Dane. Show me how you make love to our Joy. Let me see what it was like when you two were together earlier."

Dane smiled down at her as he got into position, taking up the special place he had before. He fit there so perfectly, it felt like coming home. Joy wished she could hug him, but she knew better than to move her hands from where Walker had put them.

This time, Dane entered her easily. He didn't have to work for it. He simply slid inside and took up where they'd left off. His hips began to move, first in a circle, not in and out. The motion allowed her to get used to having him inside her again.

With grace and tenderness, he began to fuck her,

gently though no less effectively than Walker had. Her eyes went wide when he discovered the motion she enjoyed most and repeated it like a broken record.

So she had a clear view when Walker reached down from his position, standing at the side of the bed, and used his thumb to pry open Dane's mouth. When it was wide enough to permit his cock entrance without risking being bitten, he stepped up and planted one foot on either side of her head, in the triangle made by her arms, then very carefully crouched so that it was obvious what he intended.

Walker held Dane's head still and fed his best friend his mostly soft dick.

Dane's hips hitched, and he shoved himself a little harder into her on that return stroke. Joy moaned. It was so fucking hot to see him servicing Walker while he was buried inside her. She couldn't possibly miss a single detail from her vantage point, which she was sure was Walker's intention.

"Can you taste her pussy on me?" he asked.

Dane nodded, causing Walker's dick to fall from his lips as he struggled to multitask.

"I bet it's sweet." Walker swiped the pad of his thumb over Dane's glistening lower lip, then brought it to his own mouth.

When she heard the wet sounds of him sucking on the tip, Joy's pussy clenched around Dane's erection.

"Shit, yes." Dane groaned. Whether at Walker or her, she wasn't sure. Probably both. The three of them worked together. They complemented each other in ways she never would have imagined and certainly hadn't understood back in high school.

She craved more, another orgasm. Walker's banter

combined with Dane's gentle intrusions to make it happen. They wound her up slowly, ensuring she wrung every bit of pleasure from their actions. Fortunately, it seemed like they got the same benefit from their interactions.

Things were heating up again, like water about to boil. Tiny bubbles of pleasure began to form and rise through her blood.

"Put it in your mouth," Walker ordered.

Joy could tell he was already growing again. If Dane worked his magic, and she knew he would, Walker would be back in the game before long. He might be ready to take her again when Dane was finished getting his fill.

Could they do this all night? She'd like to find out.

"Remember, the only thing you have to do is enjoy," Walker told her as he tightened his grip on Dane's hair. His ass clenched as he began to fuck his best friend's face while Dane matched the tempo he set, except within her.

Several minutes later, she realized Dane was straining against her, trying to burrow deeper with each swing of his hips. Walker had gone quiet, which probably meant he was concentrating on prolonging the experience.

So Joy helped them both along. "Walker?"

"Yeah." Oh, yup. His voice was ragged with the strain of holding back.

"Can we try something?" She couldn't believe what she was about to ask, but it was what she desired most.

"Tell me." He didn't say no.

"I want to be between you. With both of you holding me while we make love." Because that's what they were doing. And she wanted Walker to acknowledge it too. Besides, she had to imagine that they might cling to her and never let her go again. Even if that was dangerous to hope for forever.

He didn't bother to respond, but instead climbed off her, his now erect cock waving as he maneuvered into position. And before she knew it, she was being rolled to her side.

Dane lay in front of her and Walker behind. Dane was still connected to her, still rubbing himself along her entire body, sending sparkles of pleasure through every place he touched.

Walker hugged her, wrapping her in his heat and strength.

"Take a break," he said to Dane as he reached between her legs from behind and tugged his best friend's cock from her pussy.

Dane growled and buried his face in the crook of her neck. Had he been close to coming? Or did Walker need a turn. Maybe both.

Either way, she didn't have long to wonder about it because Walker took hold of his own hard-on and guided it to her pussy. When his torso tucked tight against her ass, he cursed softly in her ear, then kissed her cheek. "I missed you."

Whether he meant since he'd been inside her or during the years they'd spent apart, she could easily say the same. "Me, too."

He clutched her to him as he began to ride her from behind, groaning when Dane took her knee and lifted it to give Walker better access. He watched them fuck for a few minutes before he dipped in to kiss her. The riot of sensations overwhelmed Joy, taking her to a place where all she could do was absorb the ecstasy they gave her.

Joy Ride

So she hardly noticed when Dane told Walker, "I need more. Let me in."

She figured they were going to swap spots again.

Instead, she felt the tip of Dane's cock nudging her folds alongside Walker. Could they…?

"Are you up for this?" Walker asked her with a hint of wistfulness that made her positive he hoped she was. "You don't have to try it."

"I had a baby. You two are big, but you're not *that* big." She laughed, though it turned strangled when Dane pinched her nipple in playful retaliation.

"Please," asked Dane again. "If I see even the slightest wince on her gorgeous face, I promise I'll stop."

Walker nodded. "Come in. I want you to fuck her with me. Let's do this together."

20

Joy reached one hand behind her to grab Walker's hip and the other sought Dane. She clung to them both, afraid to let them stray even an inch away. She needed them as badly as they needed her.

It took Dane several tries, but eventually he began to sink inside instead of slipping off his mark. Joy's eyes flew open and her mouth turned into a surprised ring as she took them both and held them together within her body.

"You're perfect, Joy. Made for us." Walker bit her shoulder as he held still, allowing Dane to settle in before they began to move.

And when they did, she screamed. Not in pain, but in pleasure.

Imagining their dicks caressing each other even as they did the same to her drove her wild. She clamped around them.

"She's going to come," Walker rasped to Dane. "Don't you dare come with her. Not yet."

Dane gritted his teeth and nodded.

They worked her until Walker's prediction came true. She lost control and tipped into climax, her sheath rippling around them, and still they fucked. They didn't give her a chance to cool down and only stoked the fire within her higher.

"Joy," Walker murmured in her ear. "Have you ever had anal sex?"

Huh? She shook her head no. If she hadn't done it with them, she hadn't done it, period.

That didn't mean she wasn't willing to try it, though.

If only she could move or make her brain respond, she'd tell him that.

"Ah, you're getting worn out finally, huh?" Walker chuckled. "That's okay, we'll try it some other time. You're going to love having my cock there while Dane takes care of your pussy."

Dane grunted. She felt the tension in his muscles when he cleared his throat.

"What is it?" she asked him, prying her eyes open as she emerged from her post orgasmic haze only to embrace reawakening desire.

Walker paused then too, narrowing his eyes as he studied their partner.

Goose bumps broke out on Dane's arms right before he reached out and put his hand on Walker's wrist. Then he said, "If that's what you're in the mood for, fuck me instead."

Walker froze, glancing between Dane and Joy.

"I take it that's not how your typical threesomes go." Joy tipped her head, wondering why Walker would balk at the suggestion when his cock clearly voted yes. It surged within her, eager to take Dane up on his offer.

"Nothing about today is typical." Dane kissed her

again, tensing his ass so he drove into her a bit deeper. "No, that's something we've only shared when we're alone. I don't know why. I guess..."

Was he ashamed that he enjoyed it? Or afraid of rejection from either their previous partners...or Walker.

"We should focus on pleasing Joy." Walker shook his head.

Disappointment flashed over Dane's face. He looked down, but not before she caught it.

"It does. Please me, I mean. To see you taking care of Dane and to watch you both getting off on the bond you share." Joy hugged Dane, trying to reassure him. She loved him even more because of how loyal he was to Walker. "Besides, I'd rather today was about the three of us than me alone. This is the first day of our future together. That only works if we're equals and we acknowledge all of our desires."

Still Walker hesitated, making Dane's cock lose some of its stiffness within her.

"Don't act like you're not tempted, Walker. Look at his tight ass. Imagine how it will feel to fuck him knowing that every time you put your cock in him, it'll drive him deeper into me." Joy wasn't sure where such dirty talk came from, but it turned out to be a very effective tool.

"Of course I'm tempted!" Walker roared. "Either of you alone is practically more than I can handle. Both of you together... I don't stand a chance, do I?"

"No," Dane and Joy said at the same time.

"Fine, but if this ends in disaster, don't blame me." Walker grimaced. "I'm not strong enough to say no anymore."

"Thank God," Dane murmured before kissing Joy as if to thank her too. How long had he needed this? To be accepted for who he was and what he preferred instead of living two separate lives where he took women with Walker but only got the rest of what he craved in private, as if he had something to hide.

Joy hoped this would be a new beginning for them, and especially for Dane. She'd be happy if they could show him, even this once, that he was amazing, exactly how he was.

Walker reached down and grabbed Dane's hips. He lifted, pulling Dane from Joy's body and removing the weight of him from her too. She whimpered and reached for him.

"I'll give him back," Walker chuckled. "As soon as you get on your hands and knees. Put your face on my pillow and that ass up high in the air."

Joy couldn't say why it aroused her to obey his commands, but it did. She complied as quickly as possible. She tilted her head to see the guys out of the corner of her eye so she didn't miss it when Dane struggled, as eager to be buried inside her again as she was to hold his cock.

Walker ran his hand down Dane's body from his pecs over his flat abdomen and then grabbed his erection. He led Dane to her by the dick and aligned his hard-on so the tip was notched in her opening.

Joy gasped and begged, "Please, let him fuck me again. I need him."

"So do I," Walker admitted.

He slapped Dane's ass, hard, the reverberation ringing around their bedroom. "Get in there. Make sure you do a good job since your tight ass is going to distract me in a minute."

"I will," Dane promised before doing as he was told.

He pressed forward, inserting himself so deeply that his torso and upper thighs cupped Joy's ass. He banded one arm around her waist to anchor her to him.

"Now, hold still." A soft plastic snick was followed by something wet and sloshy, lube she assumed, before Dane yelped and jumped, settling deeper inside her.

They both moaned.

Then Walker cursed and said, "Brace yourself."

Dane groaned and put his mouth over the marks Walker had already left on her shoulder. Where the other man had bit her, Dane soothed, licking and sucking as Walker invaded his ass. His cock twitched inside her, obviously not deterred by whatever discomfort might be accompanying the penetration.

Walker bottomed out in Dane and shoved them all forward a bit.

Dane stiffened, making Joy pulse around his cock. The poor man wasn't going to be able to hold out much longer. For that matter, neither was she.

Walker must have experienced the same desperation. "Okay, you two. Here we go. Better enjoy it while it lasts."

With that, he began to fuck. And if she thought he'd go gentle on them, she would have been mistaken. Walker gave Dane everything he'd asked for and more. He drilled into Dane, which caused his best friend to lunge into her. With his motions, he fucked them both.

And when Dane let his hand wander to her mound, his fingers spread around his cock, she knew what he had in mind. He found her clit like he had sexual GPS in his hands then began to draw circles around it until her thighs quivered and she was afraid she would collapse.

"Walker!" Dane called.

"I feel it," Walker told him before smacking his ass.

"Let her come, and when she does, you can too. I won't be able to resist you both."

Dane began to kiss her neck in addition to whatever the hell his hand was doing. The other wandered upward to cup her breast, and she had no chance. Joy shattered around him, shocked that she could still experience such intense release after their landmark day.

It surprised her again when Dane fell too, shooting into her with a strangled cry she'd never heard from him before. She would bet he'd never come so hard in his life. Knowing she was there when he was completely fulfilled for the first time made her wring his cock even more.

Twice as much when Walker joined them, shouting their names and smacking the headboard into the shiplap walls with the ferocity of his own release. She had never imagined she would participate in something so radical yet effortless. Their love for each other and how they expressed it touched her.

It set off another round of aftershocks that milked Dane's cock dry.

"Fuck yes. I can feel you coming in me." Dane groaned and writhed between her and Walker.

Walker's hand slipped around Dane's neck, gentle despite the violence of his continuing orgasm. Whether it was to ground himself or to assert his possessive hold over Dane, she wasn't sure, but either way it was sexy as hell.

And when they'd all been wrung out, they settled. Her flat onto the mattress, unable to hold herself up even a moment longer. Dane sandwiched her to the soft covers, and Walker rested on him.

Who needed to breathe? Air was overrated compared to the heat and weight that meant they were still there with her.

Joy Ride

Dane groaned behind her and the bed shifted as Walker withdrew from his best friend and went in search of something to clean them up. She drifted while he was away, soaking in Dane's never-ending caresses and the whispered words of praise he lavished on her.

When Walker returned, he tapped Dane, encouraging the guy to roll onto his side next to her. Then her whole world turned as Walker scooped his arms under her and rotated her so that she was splayed on her back instead, with Dane pressed along her full length as he had been when he'd made love to her earlier.

Instead of a perfunctory wipe with the washcloth he'd brought with him, Walker crawled onto the bed and hovered above them, his knees planted with one between her spread legs and the other between Dane's.

It shocked her when he leaned in and lapped at the sticky trail Dane's release had left where it overflowed her pussy. The warm flat of his tongue was nearly too much on her sensitized skin, but Dane was there to hold her tight so that Walker could enjoy the proof of how much he'd pleased them both.

He worked his way closer to the source before sealing his mouth over her and penetrating her with his tongue. The hum that vibrated his whole chest and the bed beneath her ass sent similar shivers through her body.

Joy cried out and dropped her hand to his head. She speared her fingers into his hair and held on as he did his best to clean her out.

And when he was finished, he turned to Dane.

Joy moaned when he nuzzled the other man's flaccid cock before taking it into his mouth and cleaning every bit of their mingled fluids from his skin. It surprised her to see that Dane was getting hard again when Walker pulled off.

How much stamina did the man have?

He awed her. And Walker too, apparently.

"What should we do about this?" Walker asked Joy.

"Nothing." Dane tried to cover himself, but Walker was having none of it. He pinned Dane's hands at his side so that his burgeoning erection was on display. "I'm good. Seriously. This has been the best day of my sex life by far."

"No reason to stop now if you can keep breaking records." Joy smiled up at him.

"Maybe one more." Dane licked his lips. "A quick one. Just…"

"What?" she asked.

"There's another first I've always dreamed about." He looked nervously at Walker.

"You've been holding something back from me?" Walker growled. "I'll beat your ass for that later. What is it? What do you want?"

"You've never gone down on me." Dane flung his arm over his face so it was buried in the crook of his elbow. "It's fine if you're not into me like that. Into it, I mean."

Joy cut her gaze to Walker. There was no way he was going to let Dane believe that bullshit, was he? The man she loved never would.

So she shouldn't have been surprised when Walker leaned down and engulfed Dane's cock in a single, noisy slurp. He wasn't graceful or careful, but he sucked Dane off like he was a world champion.

Joy couldn't help it, she wanted to be a part of it. She reached over and cupped Dane's balls, making him whip his arm from over his face to study her reaction to his obvious bliss.

Her grin clashed with his as she kissed him ferociously, hoping he could tell how damn much he turned her on, even if her body was too tired to do anything about it for a while.

"Oh, shit. Fuck. Yeah." Dane writhed on the bed. "I'm going to—"

He jerked like he'd touched a livewire.

Walker pinned him down and slid his mouth to the base of Dane's cock, swallowing a few times before he released his best friend's cock, which softened rapidly in the wake of his epic orgasm.

"You didn't have to..." Dane pried his eyes open to look questioningly at Walker.

"I know. But I've wondered too. It never seemed right before, though. Not until today."

"You don't always have to be the strong one," Joy promised him. "We're here for you too."

"Yeah, what she said. Except I'm not moving for a year," Dane huffed.

Walker cracked up as he fell between them, gathering them both to his muscular chest and holding them tight. "Good. Because I have everything I've ever wanted, right here."

Everything except our daughter, right? Joy thought.

While it had been incredible, what they'd shared, her maternal instincts were kicking in, questioning if Arden had enough bottles or if she was fussy or if Gavyn would know what her favorite blanket was. Did it make her a terrible mom that she'd passed her baby off to their friend so that she could make love to her two soul mates for the entire day?

Probably not. But mom guilt started to creep in anyway.

"That was the most amazing thing I've ever experienced," Dane said, breaking her out of her thoughts. "When can we do it again?"

Walker ruffled his hair then said, "Not now."

"All I know is I've had more sex today than the whole rest of my life put together." Joy laughed, then turned to Dane. "I might take you up on that massage later if you're still offering."

"Yeah, of course." He smiled softly.

"Why don't you do that and I'll go get your daughter?" Walker said as he rose from the bed, stretching.

Maybe it was an innocent slip of the tongue, but it instantly set Joy on edge, erasing some of the lassitude in her bones. "What do you mean?"

"Gavyn's probably ready for some relief…" Walker trailed off when he caught the way she was looking at him in warning.

Dane cleared his throat. "I think she means you should go get *our* daughter."

At least Dane understood her even if Walker wasn't fully in agreement.

"Oh. Right." Walker scratched his chin through his beard. He had his back to them when he said, as if it were an innocent comment, "Don't you think we should get a paternity test done soon so we know who she really belongs to?"

A scalding knife stabbed Joy right in her newly unfettered heart.

Walker obliterated the warm fuzzy feelings she'd been harboring about their future and how what had happened today might make things better or at least different.

"Walker, shut the fuck up," Dane barked, his face

reminding her of when he'd charged the other man earlier. He reached for Joy, but she rolled away, then swung out of the bed.

How stupid had she been to think they were interested in being a family simply because they'd been down to get off?

"Walker, you idiot!" Dane raged as she bolted from the room. "Don't you get it? Arden is better off with three loving parents than two, no matter which two those are."

"Not if one of them has a bounty on his head," Walker hissed, though not too low for her to catch it as she crossed the hall to the bathroom.

She wouldn't risk anyone hurting her daughter the way Walker had hurt her, intentionally or not.

Arden shouldn't be allowed to learn to love him if he was only going to vanish on them when he got scared, because she now recognized that was his problem. He wasn't as tough as he'd like to be. As he pretended to be.

He'd never be able to deal with it if something bad happened because they loved him.

No amount of sex was going to fix this, because the closer they got, the more the possibility scared him.

Joy slunk into the bathroom and shut the door behind her, not with a slam but with a very quiet click. She felt defeated, emotionally abandoned if not physically, and somehow that was even worse than the times they'd vanished.

They were never going to be able to make this work.

She turned on the water to the hottest setting she could stand and attempted to scrub away any reminder of how foolishly and completely she'd given herself to someone who didn't deserve her...or *their* daughter.

21

Walker trudged across the lawn toward Hot Rides for the second time that day, even more convinced than he'd been on the first go-around that things simply weren't going to work out with him, Dane, and Joy.

Clearly, it wasn't the sex that was the problem. That part they had down.

It was everything else that was a fucking disaster.

When he got to the garage he realized that sometime during the couple of hours they'd spent in bed—and on the living room floor—the rest of the mechanics had closed up shop. There was a note on the office door that said *We're taking Arden to our house. Come over whenever you're ready...no rush! Gavyn & Amber*

Beneath that, in a distinctly messier handwriting was *No, seriously. Take your damn time. Wren, Devra, And Kyra*

Great. Walker sighed as he realized he was going to have to face a bunch of their friends, who would be eager for good news he couldn't deliver without lying. He ripped the note from the door, crumpled it in his fist, and jammed it in his pocket.

Despite the near-freezing temperatures, he still hadn't cooled off by the time he'd reached Gavyn's house. He would like to blame it on his frustration, but really, he was probably still smoldering from what he'd done with Joy and Dane.

He shouldn't have given in. Now he only had more evidence to support how spectacular it was to tangle with them and what he was going to be missing out on for the rest of his life.

Walker climbed the porch steps and rapped on the door three times before footsteps approached. Cooing and laughing and chatting—things he didn't have the heart to entertain at the moment—spilled out from inside.

"Hey," he said, expecting Gavyn to open the door to his own house. Instead, it was Tom—Eli's dad. Where he was, Ms. Brown almost certainly was too. It wouldn't be out of the realm of possibility to find any number of the Hot Rods gang hanging out with them.

Especially with two babies to snuggle under one roof. If nothing else, Arden would always be well taken care of at Hot Rides. That at least made Walker glad they'd found the place. Even if he didn't end up being able to stay.

"Uh oh." Tom grimaced. "Sunglasses in winter. I've raised enough boys to know what that means. Need some frozen peas for that shiner?"

Walker should have known he wouldn't get away with that. He took his shades off. No point if he wasn't fooling anyone. "Nah, I'm good. Any chance I could get Arden quick and sneak out without being bombarded with a million questions I don't have the answers for?"

"Sorry, son." Tom clapped a surprisingly strong hand

Joy Ride

on his upper arm and yanked him inside, slamming the door behind him. "That's not how things work around here. Come say hello to your daughter. She's been so good, but I can tell she's looking around for you three every once in a while."

Joy definitely, Dane, probably, but him? Nah, couldn't be. Could it?

Tom took off for the living room without checking to see if Walker was following. Around here, you did as Tom said. Out of respect, if not because it was required. He led by the strength of his character alone. No duress required. Unlike Walker's own father.

Yet again, he was reminded of how different Hot Rides, Hot Rods, and even the Powertools crew was from Wildfire. There were good people in the world, he just hadn't been lucky enough to be born into a family like that. He yearned for Arden to have better than the legacy he could give her.

"She's *Joy's* daughter," Walker corrected as he entered the living room, which made his tiny home seem *extra* tiny. Of course at that instant it went as quiet as the night of the New Year's Eve party when the music had cut and Joy had strutted back into his life. Along with Arden.

"Don't let *her* hear you say that, you idiot." Wren held her arms up, bent at the wrists in a gesture that clearly asked, *Are you stupid?*

Yes. Yes, he was. For thinking they'd ever had a chance.

Ms. Brown frowned and came to Tom's side. She fussed over Walker's black eye until he turned his less colorful side to her. In his peripheral vision, he realized that yes, a large part of the gang was in attendance to witness his disgrace, including Quinn, Trevon, Devra,

Wren, Jordan, Kason, Kyra, Ollie, Van, Eli, Alanso, and Sally.

And those were just the people he caught sight of before shifting his stare to the floor.

He wondered what it would be like to be unashamed of who and what he was. As the son of a murdering, drug-dealing piece of shit—who'd also probably knocked up his stepsister and definitely had screwed things up for his best friend—he suddenly felt very out of place among these decent folks.

For a little while, he'd basked in their high opinion of him. Now he remembered the multitude of reasons why he didn't deserve it.

"Why don't you come sit here for a minute and talk to Tom and me?" Ms. Brown touched his hand softly, bringing his head up again.

In her gaze he didn't see censure, rather pity. Which was almost worse.

"I'm not sure discussing things is going to help." Walker groaned. "And what we just did together sure didn't either."

"I hope you at least gave Dane some way to blow off steam other than using you as a punching bag." Alanso cursed in Spanish. "I've been him before. In love with a dominant male too stupid to take what he's offering. It takes a lot of *blowing off*—if you know what I mean—to get rid of that much frustration."

"Hey. I'm making up for it now, right?" Eli winced and knocked his shoulder into his partner's.

Mustang Sally came up behind them and hugged them both tight. "It was tough getting past those bumps, but now...we're home free."

"Keep fighting, Walker. You won't be sorry." Eli made

room for Sally to join him and Alanso. Together, the three of them were the poster children for his wildest fantasies.

"What's the problem?" Ms. Brown asked quietly.

"Joy and Dane know my father. They should understand what he's capable of and what lengths he'll go to in order to get what he wants. I'm afraid that being with me makes them—and Arden—targets. Besides, the two of them are so much...*better*...than me. In every way. They deserve to be happy and together, without me to fuck that up or drag them down to my level. Hell, I just screwed my own stepsister and loved every second of it, for god's sake. Who does that?"

Ms. Brown cringed. Though apparently not only at his language or his Hulkish mannerisms. Because she said, "Careful who you offend, dear."

"You know there was a time when I would have called Eli my brother, right?" Alanso asked, his Cuban accent thickening as it did when he got heated, not that it happened often.

"Yeah. But that's different," Walker responded reflexively.

"How?" Eli asked. "My dad adopted him. And Sally. And all the rest of the Hot Rods. And here we are, getting it on. It took me a long time to move past that too, I swear. In fact, I almost waited too long and drove Alanso away. Even after he and I stumbled across the Powertools crew leading by example, I still resisted. Don't make the same mistakes I did. Save yourself that pain. Keep Joy and Dane from experiencing it, too. Because they love you even if they haven't told you so and you *will* hurt them if you keep going down this road."

Tom and Ms. Brown nodded, beaming with pride over

their son. He'd turned into a hell of a leader. Could Walker really follow his example?

Before he could express more of his deep-seated doubts, a shrill ring cut through their conversation. Amber bounced Noah when he roused at the sound.

Walker looked to Gavyn, along with everyone else.

"That's the shop phone. I have it forwarded here after hours. Let the machine get it." Gavyn waved them off. "We have more important things to do right now. Like getting you three back on track."

Except when the answering service kicked in, the voice projected through the home automation system was familiar…yet…not quite right. The person speaking was in distress or—more likely—nervous because they were inexperienced at being a soldier in Angus's wars.

"Hi. My name is Rivet. I'm looking for some, uh, friends of mine named Joy, Walker, and Dane. I heard you might know them. I really need to talk to them."

Everyone stared at Walker. Including Gavyn, who said, "You going to get that?"

"Fuck no!" he roared. "I don't want anything to do with Angus and his pissant club members."

Rivet, one of the young up-and-coming guys—hell, hardly more than a skinny-ass boy, really—hesitated, then continued. "It's important. Please. Please tell them I need their help."

"Are you sure we can't answer that for you?" Quinn asked, clearly uncomfortable turning away someone who sounded like they were scared and probably in danger. That was exactly the reaction Angus would try to elicit.

"No fucking way." Walker sliced his hands through the air.

"There's something I need to tell them. It's urgent. I

Joy Ride

don't know how much time I have left before I have to go back or I get caught..." Another pause before Rivet continued in an even more hushed tone.

Damn, he was good at this. Angus had probably sprung for some acting lessons. Or maybe Clive was standing there with a baseball bat, threatening to break Rivet's legs if he didn't lure the three of them and Arden away from Hot Rides, where they'd been safely entrenched for weeks.

"I don't have a number where they can reach me without someone listening in. I'll try again if I can and in the meantime, I'll be at the burger joint in the center of Middletown for a couple more hours this afternoon. Then I'll have to disappear for a while, if it's not too late by then. Please. Please tell them. You're my only shot." Rivet took one last shaky breath, then hung up.

Everyone in the room gawked at Walker, waiting for him to explain.

Of course, that's when Joy must have showed up because she called from the hallway. "Walker? Is that Rivet? Is he here?"

She jogged into the room, whipping her gaze around, her hair nearly as wild as her eyes.

"No, that kid was leaving a voicemail." Kyra went to Joy and put a steadying hand on her back.

"Forget you heard that bullshit." Walker crossed his arms. "Angus is playing dirty. He knows you'll fall for Rivet's act because you're soft."

Joy lunged for him. If Trevon and Wren hadn't intervened, she probably would have blackened his other eye to prove him wrong. "I'm tougher than you think, Walker. Strong enough to say...that's it. I'm done with you. You're not the man I thought you were."

"I've been trying to tell you that for years, Joy." It still crushed him that she'd finally realized it.

"If Rivet needs help, I'm going." She stood up straighter. "I know what it's like to be desperate to escape Wildfire and that whole life. Rivet has even more reason…"

Joy glanced around the room as if agonizing about continuing.

"We can help if you let us," Jordan told Joy. "Between Van and me, we have the training and the contacts. What can we do?"

"I'm not sure. But it's not safe for Rivet to stay at Wildfire. If he says he needs help, we have to believe him. I can't live with the consequences otherwise." Joy glanced wistfully toward Arden, wrapped in Devra's arms. "Call Dane to come for Arden. Maybe you all should go over to Hot Rods and hang out for a while with him and the babies. Take Walker too. Stay together."

"Where the hell do you think you're going?" Walker asked, marching toward her.

"To get Rivet."

"Think, Joy!" Walker shouted at her. "Think instead of always following your damn heart, which gets you in trouble. No way are we going to give Angus a shot at you, or Arden through you. And we're sure as hell not bringing Rivet back here so he can spy on us for my father. Absolutely not."

"If I'm not welcome to come home with Rivet, I'll find somewhere else to go." Joy's mouth was pinched, as if the thought was as distasteful to her as it was to him. "I'll leave Arden until I'm sure this isn't some kind of trap."

"Why? Why do you care so much about Angus's fucking errand boy?" He tried not to be jealous. After all,

Joy Ride

he'd believed Joy when she said she'd only ever chosen to be with him and Dane. So what was her attachment to the young man?

"Because there's something you don't know. Rivet wasn't lying about that." Joy scrubbed her hand over her face as if it was hard to even say out loud. What secrets had she been hiding for the guy? Would it be such a betrayal to admit it now?

"Tell me," he commanded.

Joy blurted, "Rivet isn't a *he*. Rivet is a *she*. If Wildfire finds out, your father will kill her or have Clive do it for him. You know he will!"

22

Joy couldn't believe what she'd just heard. Her guts twisted as she imagined Rivet out there, scared and alone. And in danger. Exactly like Joy had been before she'd crashed the party at Hot Rides and forced her way back into Walker and Dane's lives. Maybe that had been her mistake.

How could she expect them to welcome her into their world when she'd thrust herself on them without a choice after they'd made it very clear they wanted to start fresh, without any reminders of the past?

Still, if something happened to Rivet, like the brutality Joy had survived—or worse—she would never forgive Walker. Or herself. There was no way in hell she was going to sit by without taking action simply because Walker said so. Fuck that. Fuck him.

What was the use of having freedom if she didn't make the choices she believed were right?

She hoped Rivet would forgive her for spilling her secret, but it was the only chance she had to persuade Walker to do the decent thing. Surely no matter how twisted his perspective had become lately, he wouldn't be able to turn his back on someone who had in effect been like extended family to him. Did those bonds, and the ones he had with her, really mean nothing to him simply because of where he'd formed them?

Especially when he himself understood what it was like to try to evade the slimy tentacles of Wildfire's reach, which kept threatening to draw you back under.

"Rivet's a what?" Walker practically shouted.

"A woman," Joy confirmed.

"Like trans? Or like…what exactly?" He tugged on his beard. "My father isn't exactly tolerant, you know."

"Yeah, I get that. But no, I think she's cis. Posing as a man for some reason she didn't get a chance to tell me after she exposed herself to me—quite literally—while hiding it from Angus and the rest of the club. I don't know what game she's playing at. It's gone on too long now. You know as well as I do, if anyone finds out…" Joy wrung her fingers just imagining the consequences for breaking the rules and making a fool out of the rest of the Wildfire members. They wouldn't see it as a laughing matter.

"Son of a bitch! Wildfire doesn't allow women in the clubhouse, never mind as active members in the organization." Walker punched his palm. "What is he…I mean, *she*…playing at?"

"I honestly don't know." Joy shrugged. "I was too scared to ask her about it anywhere near Angus's property and never had a chance to speak to her alone after she tipped me off. But it doesn't matter. I'm going to find her."

"No, you're not." Walker stepped closer and extended his hand as if he'd hold her in place.

Joy slapped it away. "Don't touch me. You don't have that right anymore."

Walker jerked as if she'd smacked his bruised face instead of his fingers. "You value her life over your own?"

"Of course." Joy looked at him like he was nuts. "No one has ever stood by me and refused to abandon me when I needed them most. I will never turn my back on someone who's counting on me. Never. I might not be a lot, but I'm all Rivet has. If it was you, even now, I'd be there for you too."

She shut her eyes and swallowed hard. He didn't even try to make excuses or explain his point of view. Instead, he went for a low blow.

"*Arden* needs you," Walker insisted.

"She has Dane." Joy swiped at her eyes, which watered despite her best attempts to be stoic. "And I thought she had you too. Maybe with me out of the picture, the two of you can go back to being happy. Keep our daughter safe. Please. That's the one thing I'm asking of you."

"And I'm asking you to stay." Walker almost had her, until he added, "Not for my sake, but for your daughter's."

Your daughter's. There it was again.

"You know what? I thought you were someone else. Someone who would stand up for an innocent person in danger and someone who would love a child of mine no matter who her father was." Joy drew the slim package from her back pocket. She strode forward and shoved it into his gut so he had to grab it to keep it from tumbling to the floor. "Here. Have this. It's a paternity test. I already collected a sample from Arden, and Dane gave me his too. You should take it. Then you'll know how guilty you need to feel for the rest of your miserable life about turning your back on us. Again."

"Joy, that's..." Walker stopped before he could tell her she was being unfair.

"I'll save you the trouble of running away this time and do it for you." Joy looked around at the people gathered there, who were staring in rare silence as her life imploded. "I'll miss you guys. Thank you for everything. Please take care of my daughter until I can come back for her. If I can…"

Joy choked, then took a step backward and then another before spinning on her heel. She was about to disappear from Walker's life forever.

He seemed too stunned, or maybe petrified, about the test to say or do a damn thing about it.

"Joy, wait…" Jordan tried to reason with her, but she wasn't having it. "Let's come up with a plan. We can round up some other people from Van's security staff to go with us."

If she stayed she might be too late, or she might let them convince her that she was being foolish when she knew she was—for once in her life—doing the right thing. Taking action instead of standing by, letting the rest of the world decide her fate.

That was the old Joy. This was the new Joy.

"Rivet might not have that kind of time. You can catch up if you really care to, but I'd rather you didn't get involved in our mess." With that, Joy sprinted for the door and toward Hot Rides, where her motorcycle was stored. It was a hell of a lot faster than her mini, electric mom-mobile.

She punched in the code to the side door and ducked under the rolling aluminum as soon as it was high enough off the ground for her to limbo under. By the time she'd strapped on her helmet and gloves then started the bike, she was clear to go.

Joy leaned forward, glad that even if they were terrible

soul mates, Dane and Walker were excellent mechanics. Her café racer streaked along the blacktop driveway, shooting her toward Middletown and, hopefully, Rivet.

Please don't let me be too late!

As she sped past Gavyn's house, she tried not to look. When she did anyway, she caught a glimpse of Walker standing there, his hands on the railing, his head hung while a random assortment of their friends surrounded him. Whether they were trying to soothe him or scold him, she couldn't tell.

Van and Jordan leapt down the stairs and dashed toward Van's monster black truck. They were probably going to mobilize the security team like they'd suggested. But they were headquartered at Kason's mountain lodge on the other side of Lake Logan.

Too far away to wait for.

It might be that she'd end up with some help eventually. But life had taught her not to count on it. Not even from the men she thought she could trust the most. She should have known better than to fall in love with them all over again. They weren't made for commitment —well, maybe to each other, but not to her and, apparently, not to Arden either.

This time she vowed to learn that lesson for good.

23

When Dane heard the distinct purr of Joy's motorcycle speeding away from Hot Rides —and him—he had a sick feeling something had gone horribly wrong. Even more wrong than when Joy had emerged from their bathroom with red-rimmed eyes and insisted he swab his cheek for her damned paternity test.

Unwilling to sit around and wait for her and Walker to duke it out on their own, lest he be sitting there until he rotted, he bolted.

He didn't even bother to shut the door as he took off after Joy, tearing along the path toward Gavyn and Amber's house, where he could see a small crowd gathering on the porch. On the way, Jordan and Van rushed past him in the opposite direction.

Instead of pausing to talk, Van shouted at him, "We're going to get some more help!"

"For what?" Dane's heart raced. Was something wrong with Arden?

He stumbled but kept going, pumping his arms to

propel his run into a sprint as he headed toward Walker. His best friend was clinging to the railing of Gavyn's porch as if he'd slammed an entire fifth of whiskey and needed the grip to keep the world from spinning off its axis.

"What's wrong?" he hollered when he was close enough for anyone to hear. "Where did Joy go?"

Wren looked nervously at Kason as Trevon did the same to Quinn. Nobody was talking.

"Come on. Somebody...anybody! Fucking tell me what's happening." He charged up the stairs and crashed into Walker, threatening to take them both to the ground again.

Except his friend was limp, completely without the will to fight. He absorbed the impact and stumbled back a few steps instead of resisting or clashing with Dane.

Nothing had ever terrified him more.

Walker was officially broken.

"What did you do?" he shouted as he fisted his hands in Walker's shirt and shook the man.

"Nothing." He swallowed convulsively as if he might be sick. "I did nothing. I let her go."

When Walker opened his hand, Dane saw he was staring down at the paternity test Joy had sprung on him not that long ago. Had it shredded Walker's heart, as it had his, to think he might not have the honor of being called Arden's dad for much longer?

Walker shrugged free of Dane's hold, reached into the pouch, and took out the unused vial. "What am I supposed to do, Dane?"

He wondered if his friend was asking about the test or something a hell of a lot bigger in the grand scheme of things. Dane didn't have answers to the difficult shit so he stuck to the simple stuff.

"Swipe the inside of your cheek with that thing attached to the vial lid and put it back on." Dane pointed at the prepaid label on the front of the package. "She has it ready to mail and everything. Seal it in there with the other two, and send it off. She said we'll know in a few days. Or...you could, you know, skip it, man up, and take care of what's yours. Arden *and* Joy."

Fuck it, why stop there?

"And me," Dane murmured.

Walker's head snapped up then. He took one look at the misery that must have shone through Dane's eyes, cursed violently, then swabbed his cheek so hard Dane was afraid the thing would either snap or pierce Walker's face. When it was done, he tucked it into the vial, closed the bag, handed it to Tom, and said, "Will you mail this?"

"Of course," the older man said, though he didn't seem excited by the prospect.

"Why can't you do it your damn self?" Dane wondered, both pissed off and utterly disappointed.

"I've got somewhere else to go." Walker looked at Tom again. "That's the right thing to do, isn't it?

Tom stepped closer. "Fear of what might happen led you here. It doesn't seem like those decisions are sitting well with you at the moment. So I suggest you deal with what's actually wrong and leave the what-ifs behind. Terrible things happen to every one of us eventually. All you can do is enjoy the joy rides between the rough patches."

"So you're saying I'm being an idiot and about to miss my chance for any of the good shit in life?" Walker groaned.

"We all have our moments." Tom's smile was short-lived. "But this isn't the time to keep screwing up. The people you care about need you—Joy, Dane, Arden, me, all of us. We know the man you are capable of being. Don't let us down."

Walker nodded. "I'm going after Joy. Dane, you should stay here with Arden. Just in case...she'll need at least one of her parents."

"What am I missing?" Dane flicked his stare between Tom and Walker, searching for a clue.

"Rivet called. Either Angus is setting us up or Rivet needs our help." Walker sighed.

"So Joy went? Alone?" Dane's fingers went icy cold, and not only because he'd rushed out of the house without his gloves. "What the hell is wrong with you? Why would you let her do that?"

"I clearly can't control what she does." Walker huffed at that. "Also...Rivet is a girl."

"What?" Dane nearly fell on his face again. No way. The guy was a runt, sure. But...a woman? No way he would have been able to tell. This *had* to be one of Angus's tricks. And Joy was facing it by herself.

Walker shrugged. "According to Joy, who refused to explain how exactly she knew that or why Rivet would hide that factoid..."

"And you seriously stood there and let Joy leave to get twisted up in the middle of that clusterfuck? What the hell is wrong with you?" Dane yelled. "If something happens to her, I swear to God I'll cut your balls off with a rusty knife and run your dick through the power hammer."

"Remind me never to make him mad," Quinn muttered from beside them.

Dane was not amused. "I've already let her down so

many times. If she gets hurt again and I'm not there to do anything about it…"

"You're right. I'm an idiot. I should have thought about how that would haunt you…us. Okay, fine, us. I can't do it either." Walker grabbed Dane's arm and tugged. "Let's go. If we floor it, we might not be that far behind her. And if it does turn out to be a setup, I'm eager to take my turn at kicking someone's ass."

Tom nodded and smiled at Walker then. "That's the way, son. Be careful, both of you. And hurry home with those girls."

Side by side, Walker and Dane ran to the garage and the storage bay where they parked their motorcycles. Conveniently, Joy had left it open. As they straddled their motorcycles and grabbed their helmets, Dane said, "Walker, you know we're better together than apart. Safer too. You can't control everything. You're going to have to learn how to live with uncertainty."

"Can we talk about this later?" Walker grimaced.

"Just in case there isn't a later, I need you to know that I love you. And that I want a life with you and Joy, raising our daughter and hopefully more kids together, even if you two are both royal pains in my ass." He slammed down his visor and started his bike, the roar drowning out anything Walker might have said in return.

Then he was off, barreling down the long, winding driveway through the woods, with Walker right beside him, where he belonged. Dane didn't even know where they were headed, but as long as Walker was leading the way and Joy was wherever they ended up, he would gladly follow.

24

They made it to Middletown in record time, with Walker signaling Dane to pull up behind his favorite burger restaurant. Great, now they were going to cause a scene and he'd be banned for life, no more quarter pounds of greasy heaven for him.

They cut their engines more than a block away and rolled into the alley near the dumpsters, but nobody from Wildfire would be fooled by that stunt. If there were club members around, they knew Walker and Dane had arrived.

So they couldn't be subtle. There was nothing for it but to bust in and see what was up.

Walker and Dane marched together, looking every direction possible. They fell into their old routines, ones they'd learned from Wildfire and perfected in their time in the service.

When they reached a window, Dane ducked low and surveyed the restaurant. There, in the back corner, he saw Joy's familiar silhouette. The person across from her was one he didn't recognize, though. With long obsidian hair, manicured nails, and some seriously glossy lipstick, the woman sharing the booth with Joy was beautiful and high maintenance.

Could *that* be Rivet? No fucking way.

"It's clear," he told Walker when he finished scanning the restaurant and saw nothing alarming. At least not for the moment. They had to get Joy, whoever the fuck she was meeting with, and get the hell out before they were trapped inside and innocent people got hurt.

"Let's go." Walker gestured with his head toward the front door.

Walker and Dane stormed into the restaurant, drawing a number of stares when they nearly caused the door to rip off its hinges in their urgency. Dane followed two steps behind as Walker barreled down the aisle and dropped into the booth beside Joy. With only one place to sit, he took the empty spot next to…

The woman turned toward him and he nearly swallowed his tongue. "Rivet? Is that really you?"

She smiled before tossing long gently curled tresses over her shoulder. "Hey, Dane. I figured the best disguise would be to come in full-on woman-mode. They're not looking for that. Maybe you'd better call me Sevan instead, just in case. How do you like my wig?"

Holy fucking shit. It really was him. No, *her*, he thought. If he hadn't known, he never in a million years would have guessed that Rivet was hiding under all that hair and makeup. "It's…uh…kind of hot. Am I supposed to admit that?"

Joy laughed. The warm, ringing peal was the most beautiful thing he'd ever heard. Maybe she didn't hate him and Walker after all?

"Sure, thanks." Was Sevan seriously about to blush?

Joy Ride

His mind was blown. How the hell had he known this woman since she was pretty much still a girl and never once suspected that the merciless biker-in-training wasn't who he'd been led to believe she was?

"How's the reunion going?" Walker asked Joy.

"You trust my opinion?" Joy asked with an arched brow.

Dane kicked Walker under the table. He couldn't be allowed to fuck this up again. They might already be out of chances.

"Yes, I do." Walker turned to her and lowered his voice. "I'm sorry if I made you feel otherwise. It's always been my own judgment that I question. Lusting after a woman who's supposed to be my sister, betraying my best friend with my desires, allowing you to be hurt by my father and the people he exposed you to... It's *me* I'm ashamed of, *me* I don't trust, not you. Never you. That's why I'm afraid to call Arden my own—because I'm damn sure I don't deserve to be her dad."

Joy stared in shock. She didn't say anything, but Sevan did. "Whoa. That was heavy. And...pretty damn heartfelt. When the hell did you learn to get in touch with your feelings and shit? Angus would have a coronary if he heard you talking to your old lady like that."

"I guess becoming part of the Hot Rides family has made me weak." Walker shrugged. Dane knew it was exactly the opposite. "Now, can we please take this back to the shop where we can catch up in private, with a hell of a lot more precautions against unwanted visitors in place?"

The bell on the door rang and Dane's face fell. "Too late."

He and Walker shot to their feet at the same time, but there was nowhere to run. They were stuck in the booth at the back corner of the restaurant while Clive and two other guys he recognized from Wildfire approached, flanking the bastard.

It figured they'd sent the sergeant-at-arms to retrieve their rogue member.

"Isn't this a cozy double date?" The guy smirked, scanning first Joy and then Sevan head to toe. "Our intel didn't say anything about the three of you being here, but it makes sense now. When is Rivet supposed to show? Soon, I hope. Mind if I pull up a chair and wait with you all?"

Dane clenched his fists. He didn't give a fuck if his fingers were already bruised and cut. They were still capable of doing plenty of damage. Anything it took to give Joy and Sevan a chance to escape.

But first, he would try to talk his way out of the impending disaster. Maybe they'd get lucky and Clive would be smart enough not to start shit in such a public place. "As you can see, you're interrupting. Better wise up and head out of town."

Clive laughed. "I don't think Walker's father would like that very much. He's pissed enough that Joy and her spawn are still roaming loose. If I lose Rivet too, well, I'd be better off not going back. Where is that fucker anyway? I thought he would have been here by now."

"Guess he got cold feet." Dane shrugged. If Clive didn't recognize the woman in her natural state, he sure as fuck wasn't about to tip the guy off. "Or maybe he's just late."

Walker tried to reason with Clive. "What are you getting out of this? Aren't you tired of doing Angus's dirty work? Maybe you should start thinking about the long term."

"Oh, I am." Clive grinned, flashing one crooked gold

Joy Ride

tooth. "If I recover any of you, or eliminate you, Angus will make good on his promise."

"What the hell did he tell you that has you pretending you have balls of your own after years spent up his ass?" Walker snorted. "That he's going to promote you? Make you president when he's done? I hope you're smarter than that. Everyone knows Gunner is his pick."

Clive didn't take the bait, but a muscle in his jaw twitched. "You used to be, until you turned into a pussy. Now...yeah, it's going to be me to lead Wildfire, and Joy has always been perfect old lady material. I think the only reason your dad didn't claim her for himself was to have a chance at tempting you to come home. If you're retired for good... Well, let's just say I'd be gracious enough to ensure she has a place there—with me—after we teach her a lesson or two about trying to run away."

Walker might have taken a swing at him right then if Dane wasn't there to snag his elbow.

Clive only laughed. "We can take this outside or we can make a mess in here. I don't give a fuck."

As if to prove his point, he bent to the left and kicked out with his right foot, toppling the table beside their booth. A woman at a nearby booth screamed as silverware and glasses flew through the air, then rained to the ground with a clatter of epic proportions.

The two guys behind Clive cracked their knuckles.

And then there was no choice. They advanced.

Walker looked at Dane and nodded. Together, they charged. They met Clive and his cronies past halfway to keep them as far from Joy and Sevan as possible. It wasn't much, but hopefully it would be enough.

Walker and Dane could easily handle three men between them, as long as they didn't have...

One of the guys pulled a wicked-looking knife out of his sleeve and the other drew a gun from the waistband of his jeans.

Patrons trampled each other in their haste to abandon the diner, screaming about a shooter as they left. Dane hoped they made it out before someone got killed. He eyed the row of plate glass windows that started a few booths away from the back wall and wondered if he could throw a chair through it so Joy and Sevan could take off too.

But he didn't have a chance to try out his plan.

Clive went for Walker and the other two guys came for him.

He dodged the knife aimed straight at his heart, then clotheslined the guy holding it before kicking behind him at the other assailant, connecting with the bastard's knee.

Meanwhile, Walker was doing a similar dance with Clive. Dane had to trust that his best friend could hold his own. So he ignored their grunts and curses and the thud of flesh on flesh as he leveled the man with the knife. Unfortunately, the other bastard was right there to smash a napkin dispenser in between his shoulder blades, knocking him to his knees on the ground.

Joy shrieked as Sevan prevented her from joining the fray.

The guy lifted the gleaming dispenser again. And just went Dane thought it was over, he heard the bell on the front door ring.

Who the fuck was crazy enough to come inside? Hopefully not more Wildfire members or they would be done for. Instead, he heard Quinn say loudly, "Hey, guys! There you are. I thought you could use some company."

"They have a gun, and knives," Walker choked out

despite Clive's pressure on his windpipe. He had Walker trapped up against the wall as he used Joy's safety as a bargaining chip to keep Walker from lashing out and crushing him. If it weren't for the wreckage of the tables, and the guy with the gun, Joy and Sevan might have been able to dart past them.

"That's okay," Trevon chimed in. "You have a whole bunch of pissed-off biker friends. Us. That's far more dangerous. Plus, the cops will be here any minute. Jordan and Van are bringing some of their guys, too. Don't worry, we've got your backs. These assholes aren't going to get away with this."

Clive glanced up then, taking in Quinn, Trevon, Wren, and Alanso stalking toward them. Six to three was bad enough odds. Cops and other backup on the way would ruin his day. The only thing worse would be if he let both Joy and Sevan—even if he didn't yet realize she was Rivet—get away. Then the cops would look like toy soldiers compared to Angus and what he would order done to Clive, while he was rotting in jail or not.

Clive looked dead into Walker's eyes and, and said to the man with the gun, "Shoot him."

The assassination attempt fell short when the kitchen door was kicked open and Van barreled through it like a freight train, tackling the asshole pointing the gun at Walker. It flew out of his hands and Joy ran over to grab it while Jordan and five other guys dressed in black streamed in behind Van, assault rifles drawn, aimed at the three Wildfire members.

"We'll take it from here, guys." Jordan seemed unfazed, almost cold, as he approached Clive and twisted his arm behind his back.

"What the fuck is this?" Clive asked, frantically trying

to break free of Jordan's grasp an instant before cuffs were slapped on him.

"A favor for the cops, who should be here any moment. You're going to make quite a present for them. Now they owe me." His stone-faced response made Dane aware that despite his prior deference, he'd underestimated the guy. Badly. Jordan wasn't someone to fuck with.

"You're arresting me? Jesus. You might as well kill me right now. It would be kinder if you put a bullet between my eyes."

Walker winced, because it was true. They knew what happened to a potential leak in jail.

Dane didn't give a fuck. Clive deserved that and more. So much more. "No mercy, Clive. Not for you. Never."

Joy rushed to Dane's side and hugged him tight. They clung to each other as Clive was hauled away, struggling and cursing them. His two goons went next, with significantly fewer objections.

Walker sagged against the wall and stared at Dane and Joy, huddled together.

Dane watched right back, willing him to come closer, sure this was the moment that would decide their fate. Joy looked up too, and the unshed tears in her eyes overflowed, rolling down her cheeks. "Thank you for coming. I should have trusted your judgment but…"

"You couldn't leave Sevan to face them alone." Walker crossed to them and fell onto his knees at their feet. "I wouldn't love you so damn much if you had it in you to do that, Joy."

She began to tremble in Dane's embrace. He rubbed her arms, trying to erase the goose bumps there even if he wasn't sure of the outcome himself yet. No matter what, he would always be there for Joy. He only hoped that Walker would be there for them both, too.

"What are you saying?" she asked Walker point blank.

"I'm begging you to come home with me—with us—to Hot Rides so we can figure out how to make things work between Dane, you, and me. I want us to be the family we were always meant to be. Especially now that we have *our* daughter to worry about too."

Joy took an enormous breath, then let it out in a mixture of tears and laughter that only encouraged Dane to cling tighter to her and the pure sunshine she brought to even their darkest days. If he had his way, he'd never let go of her again.

Joy looked over her shoulder and said, "Sevan, you coming?"

"Oh hell yes. I can't wait to meet my...I mean, your daughter." The woman's smile faltered for a moment before she spent an inordinate amount of time straightening her already perfect hair.

If there was something off about Sevan, they'd deal with it together.

Much later.

25

"Is it okay if I call you Sevan?" ex-special agent Jordan Mikalski asked as he leaned forward, his elbows on his knees. Even if she hadn't heard it from Walker, she would have known he was some kind of cop.

Despite being supposedly retired, he still reeked of authority and a love of the rules.

Something she had never valued much. "Yeah, I prefer that. Never know who's listening, especially since I'm not done with my work at Wildfire."

Of course, Joy had to choose right then to walk into the great room of the fancy-ass mountain retreat where they'd stashed her. It might as well have been a fortress, built of stones and timbers the size of telephone poles, set on top of a mountain with miles of empty, gated land in every direction and guards stationed at the gates.

The place belonged to Jordan's wife's husband, Kason Cox. Yeah, that was a brainteaser and a tongue twister, but once Sevan had worked it out she realized that Walker, Dane, and Joy had found shelter here for a reason. The Hot Rides were some freaky folks.

She liked them already.

Still, who knew country stars lived like this?

Sevan supposed she should have, but she'd never thought of it before.

This was a whole different universe than she was used to. No poverty like what she'd been steeped in during her life before Wildfire. No president telling her what to do. No rival club threatening civil war at any moment. No misogynistic bullshit about what women were capable of. Hell, Wren—Jordan's wife—was a welder at Hot Rides, and Kyra—their friend—was the drummer in Kason's band.

As much as she would love to live like they did, she couldn't. Not until she'd fulfilled her purpose.

"Wait, what was that?" Joy asked, one hand propped on her hip and the other wrapped around a tiny little baby with her bright eyes. Holy shit. That was a lot of responsibility right there. "Why the hell would you even consider going back to Wildfire? I told you, you can stay with us. Or, if you don't like that idea, I'll ask Devra for an advance on my salary and help you get set up in town, although I think you're safer close by—"

"Joy, hang on a second." Sevan stood and crossed to the woman she'd always looked up to. She peered at the child in Joy's arms and sighed. It hadn't even occurred to her to hope for something like that. A real family. A future. Wow.

Sevan shook her head to keep from getting distracted by her thoughts, surprised when the ends of her wig slapped her elbows. It felt so fucking weird to have long hair, though she had been glad she'd donned her disguise when Clive had looked right past her in the diner.

Apparently the YouTube videos she'd watched on

contouring had been pretty damn effective, too, changing the entire structure of her face enough to throw him off.

"I'm sorry if I gave you the wrong idea. I didn't come here to break free. I'm looking for reinforcements. And I think I found them..."

"I'm not going back." Joy looked at her as if she was a raving lunatic. "And neither are Walker and Dane. I'm sorry. I want to help you but that's not the way. Not for any of us."

"I would never ask you to." Sevan sighed. "There's a lot you don't understand."

It weighed on her, making her even more tired that she already was.

For Sevan, it had been an endless night filled with grueling questions volleyed at her by various law enforcement agencies and a few unnamed organizations, like the one Jordan had told her he'd recently formed. However, it seemed like Joy, Walker, and Dane—the guys both following right behind her, of course—had spent that time in much more pleasurable pursuits.

Good for them. They seemed genuinely happy.

And if Sevan had even the faintest glimmer of a hope that she could pull that off someday, she had to come clean with them right then.

"Could you guys sit down so we can talk about some stuff?" Sevan asked, waving them over to the giant couches that felt as luxurious as lounging on clouds compared to the beat-up leather sofas at the Wildfire clubhouse or the threadbare sofas at her grandparents' house, which had always resulted in a spring gouging her ass when she sat on them. Hell, even the floor had been more comfortable.

"Sure, as long as you get around to why you might not

stay." Joy squeezed Sevan's hand. "I don't want you to go. I always enjoyed our talks, and I felt like we had a connection. Now I'm guessing there's plenty more we could have shared if you had let me in. It's not too late."

"Okay, so…hear me out before you say nice shit, okay?" Sevan's throat grew hoarse as she considered what her revelations might do to the only true friendship she had in the world.

Joy could very well hate her before it was done. And she wouldn't blame the woman.

"I'm too happy to be in a bad mood today." Joy beamed at Walker and Dane, who took a seat on either side of her, close enough that their thighs touched all the way down to her knees.

Oh yeah, they'd had one hell of a party last night.

Jordan was staring at Sevan, wondering about what she was about to reveal. She shrugged in lieu of apologizing for not spilling all of her sordid secrets to him when they'd been strategizing about one very specific thing: how to take down Wildfire, for good.

So she looked directly back at him and said, "You can turn on your recorder thingy. You should get this on tape in case I'm not here to tell this to a judge someday."

Jordan nodded. He took the device from his pocket, set it on the table, and pressed record like he'd done earlier when she'd relayed juicy details about Angus and what he'd been up to lately.

"I'm sorry, Walker." She bit her lip, then said in a rush, "But I think your father is evil."

"That makes two of us." He shrugged as if it wasn't a big deal, but she knew it had to hurt.

"I hate him because he murdered my mother." Sevan dug her fake fingernails into her palms, glad for the stabbing pain that distracted her from the tears welling when she finally, after all this time, said it out loud.

"Oh no. I'm so sorry, Sevan." Joy leaned forward and Arden began to fuss as if she could sense her mother's distress. Hell, she probably could.

"Son of a bitch!" Walker stared up at the ceiling for at least five seconds and Dane simply watched her, waiting for her to continue, but the pity in his gaze hit her hard.

"How?" Jordan winced. "I'm sorry to be so crude, but it'll be best if you give me as many details as you have."

Sevan drew a deep breath, fully aware that what she was about to say would damn her too. Especially in Joy's eyes. She might no longer be welcome in this sanctuary she'd stumbled across. If she didn't do it, Sevan would be equally as bad as the rest of people who'd tried to obscure the truth. "Her husband, my stepfather, found out that she'd cheated on him. They got in a huge fight, and she took off in the rain on his motorcycle. They said it was an accident, when she wrapped it around a tree, but it wasn't."

Joy sat ramrod straight. Dane clutched her free hand and Walker cursed.

"What aren't you saying?" Jordan asked, tipping his head.

Joy answered for her. "*My* mother died in a freak motorcycle accident. She wrapped Angus's motorcycle around a tree. They said she didn't know how to ride and that she never should have taken such a big bike when she was so petite. Especially not in the rain—"

Her face crumpled and she turned to Dane, burying her face against his chest as the memories overwhelmed her.

Walker, however, was still staring at Sevan. "Does that mean that you and Joy…"

Rivet nodded tightly. "We're sisters. Half-sisters, actually. I have no idea who my father is since our maternal grandparents raised me. Our mother was only with him for a short time, when she broke up with Angus in some kind of power play to try to convince him to leave Walker's mother. She'd already had Joy, so he knew about her. And when he rose to power at Wildfire, he lured my mother back. Joy was six then. He thought she'd been faithful, so she left me behind and pretended I didn't exist. He toyed with her for nearly ten years after that, keeping her as his mistress before Walker's mom disappeared. They finally got married shortly after that, and she moved in to Walker's house with Joy. I think it was after our grandmother died, when our grandfather got sick that he sent our mom a letter—because I was only fourteen and there was no one else to look after me. Of course Angus read it. That's how he found out about me. And what he saw as a betrayal. If she could lie to him about something so important for so long, he knew he couldn't trust her."

"So he got rid of her." Walker looked like he might be sick.

Sevan nodded, her guts twisting. "It's my fault that our mother is gone. If Angus hadn't found out that she'd had me…shit… I'm so sorry, Joy."

For a moment, no one responded. And when they did, it wasn't with the vile denouncements she'd expected.

"No wonder you're so beautiful, Sevan," Dane said softly as he stroked Joy's hair. It was clear that he loved her as much as he ever had. No, more. Because he was glued to her side and Sevan couldn't imagine them ever leaving her behind again. Must be nice.

Joy Ride

Joy sniffled and rose up. She handed her baby to Dane, then approached Sevan.

She fully expected a slap across the face or a tirade that ended with being ordered to leave immediately. Instead, Joy bent down and wrapped her in the warmest hug she'd ever received. "You're not responsible for anything Mom did. I loved her, of course I did, but she didn't always make the best decisions."

"That's putting it mildly." Walker frowned. "She got mixed up with my father, got hooked on his money and power, and look what happened to you both—not to mention her—because of it."

"So you don't hate me?" Sevan hadn't even allowed herself to consider that possibility.

"Of course not." Joy hugged her again. "I wish you'd told me sooner. I never would have gone without you. Family means everything to me. We need to stick together."

"I wasn't ready to leave. And I'm not staying away now either." Rivet shook her head and stared at Jordan, begging him not to rescind his offer.

"Now you're sounding more like your mom." Walker looked at her as if she'd said the wildest thing yet, and considering they'd recently found out she didn't actually have a dick and that she and Joy were long-lost siblings, that was saying a lot.

"Why?" Joy took both of Sevan's hands in hers and squeezed. "Why would you do that?"

"Simple." Sevan's spine stiffened as she vowed again to follow through on what she'd resolved to do so long ago. Now that there was an easy out, a cushy life waiting on the other side, that didn't mean she could give up. Not until

Angus paid. She finally had a real chance at bringing him to justice. "Revenge."

"That's no reason to risk your safety." Joy murmured to her, "Putting yourself in danger won't bring her back. They have Clive in custody. If they can pin the murder on him, he'll roll, you know he will. He's a slimy bastard. He'll rat on Angus in exchange for a deal."

"I agree with you to some extent," Jordan came to her rescue. "If we could get Clive to testify, that would be a major win. But building this case could take years, and let's be honest, the odds of him making it to a court date alive are slim to none."

Walker cursed, Dane looked away. Joy put her face in her hands.

They all knew it was true.

"Okay, so what's your plan?" Joy rubbed her eyes, then looked at Sevan. "You have a really good one, right? I don't want to lose my only sister, now that I know I have one."

Sevan's guts knotted, and for the first time, she doubted she was doing the right thing.

"We do." Jordan cleared his throat, then very deliberately turned off his recorder. "Nobody freak out, okay?"

"About what?" Walker wasn't making any promises. Even now that they were sort of on the same side again, Sevan was still sort of afraid of him. He was a lot like his father, if also worlds apart. If he felt she was threatening his woman, or his man, or their child... Yeah, she wouldn't survive that.

"And definitely don't kill them, okay? I need them," Jordan said, then raised his voice to add, "Hey, Van, you can bring our guests out."

And within a few seconds, the handsome, dark-haired

Joy Ride

asshole from the diner who'd nearly shot Walker stepped out of the back, escorted by the hulk of a guy they called Van. Jordan must not have turned him over to the authorities with Clive.

Along with them was…fuck her life…Levi Jansen.

Him? Why him? Jordan couldn't possibly expect her to work with him.

Then again, Jordan probably didn't know about the time Levi had kissed the shit out her in the clubhouse bathroom, when he'd thought she was a boy.

Maybe Joy was right. Sevan was in over her head. Because she'd wished she could do a hell of a lot more than make out with Levi that day, and every day since.

Tall, blond, blue eyed, calm, and intelligent, the Dutch man was nothing like most of the bikers she'd grown up around—though every bit as lethal. It was also what made him invaluable to Wildfire. No one saw his ruthlessness coming. She'd seen him take out four rival club members by himself in a deal gone wrong.

And that said nothing of what he'd done to her when he'd crushed her, telling her she wasn't man enough to handle him. Little had he known, she truly wasn't.

"What the fuck is this?" Walker roared as he shot to his feet, stepping in front of Dane and Arden. "You don't know what you're dabbling in here, Jordan."

Sevan bristled and practically hissed. If she brought trouble to Joy and her family—*more* trouble, that was—she wouldn't be able to live with it.

"Settle down, guys. That's Ransom and he's working for me now," Jordan said. "He's been partnering with Levi here for nearly two years already."

Working for…did that mean Levi was a spy? Holy fucking shit. Sevan couldn't decide if that made her despise the sneaky bastard or if she became even more infatuated with him.

"Chill out. I wasn't going to shoot you." Ransom smirked. "I've been undercover in the club for too long to screw it up. I couldn't blow my cover when I knew Jordan wasn't far behind us."

Dane flipped the guy off, but Walker was ignoring that bullshit. He asked Jordan, "What do you mean 'working for you'? I thought you retired."

"Turns out I have a new job." He shrugged.

"Yeah, you're guarding Kyra's fine ass these days," Dane said.

"I am. Most of the time. But as incredible as her ass is..." Jordan sighed. "Let's call this my side hustle."

Van spoke for him. "His talents are being wasted on my security team. This is a chance for him to do something that matters, to make up for...some shit that went down in the past."

Sevan narrowed her eyes. Could Jordan be in pursuit of a bit of revenge of his own? Now *that* she could understand.

"Turns out that although I wasn't a good fit for the ICE position, there are some 'unofficial' missions the government would like to run but can't. So JWK Consulting has been created and hired to handle their dirty work." Jordan smiled slowly and surely, and for the first time, Sevan realized that he was a hell of a lot more dangerous than she'd guessed.

She felt like she'd been dumped in the open ocean and sharks were circling closer—Angus, Levi, Jordan, and even Walker. Any of them could bite her in the ass if she didn't do this right.

Joy Ride

"You're investigating Wildfire for the RICO case?" Walker's eyes widened. "Jordan, that's serious shit."

"I know." He was solemn. "I lost my partner to this business, remember? In fact, it turns out your father is doing some business with the monsters that got Johnny killed, and I'd like to see them pay for that too."

Joy clamped her hand on Sevan's so tight she could see her sister's knuckles turn white.

Despite that, her mind was made up. Enough resources pooled together might actually have some impact. Finally. This was what she'd been waiting for. Sevan said, "I'm in."

"You just escaped!" Joy begged her, "Please don't go back. They'll hurt you like they hurt Mom."

"They didn't *hurt* her, Joy. They murdered her. And they should pay for that." She practically snarled. "All I've ever wanted was to make them pay for cutting her life short and ripping us apart. Jordan, put me back in. But this time with a chance to actually make a difference."

"Nothing you do will bring her back," Joy said gently.

Sevan sighed. "I realize you can't understand my decision, but I would hope now that you're independent, you understand what value there is in making your own choices. Respect me enough to trust me to decide on my own. I will gladly live with the consequences."

Joy opened her mouth, then shut it before nodding. "Okay, Sevan. If that's what you want. But come back soon, okay? My offer never expires. There's a place for you here, with us."

Sevan had to get the hell out of there before Joy talked her out of what she knew she had to do. She looked to Jordan. "So?"

"I'm not going to lock you out of this," he promised.

Sevan slipped her hands free of Joy's clutch, hugged the woman hard but briefly, then crossed to Levi's side. She tried to ignore the heat pouring off him and the scent of his leather jacket, which instantly reminded her of the night he'd had his tongue halfway down her throat. "When do we leave?"

"Right now," he said, and held his hand out to her. "I promise I'll take care of you as best as I can. Ransom will too. I thought you were cute as a boy, but damn."

Both of them eyed her from the tip of her toes to her long crow-black hair, pausing only to inspect the very subtle yet still-there curves at her hips, waist, and chest. That kind of attention was exactly what she'd have to avoid where they were going.

"I can take care of myself." Sevan whipped off her wig, exposing her short-cropped natural hair, and marched to the bathroom. She scrubbed the pretty makeup and fun colors from her face so hard her cheeks were red when she finished. Then she took her wicked-sharp knife from its holster in the small of her back and sliced her nails off one by one. They'd have to stop for more shapewear and Ace bandages so she could mold her body into her alternate form.

As much as she'd enjoyed the glimpse of the woman she might one day become, this was who she was and who she would remain until Angus had gone down for good—an unassuming, easily forgettable errand boy who fixed bikes for the important members of Wildfire.

Rivet was back.

26

A WEEK LATER

Joy rocked Arden in her arms, still amazed by how much life could change in an instant. Sometimes for the better, despite what she'd believed before. She smiled down at her daughter and held her tighter, closer to her heart. The baby looked up at her and gurgled happily.

"There are my pretty girls," Walker said as he came up beside them. Then he cleared his throat. "Can I hold her, Joy?"

"Of course." She handed Arden off to him without hesitation. It still made her insides mushy when she watched his big hands surround the baby with an inherent promise to protect her and love her. As he'd always tried to do for Joy and was succeeding at now.

Their near miss the week before had changed Walker, hopefully forever.

Then again, she had one last thing to settle with him and Dane before they could move forward.

She figured this was as good a time as any. So she went

into Arden's room—since she was now sharing a bed with Walker and Dane permanently, she hoped—and took the crisp white envelope from the top drawer, where she'd hidden it behind Arden's teeny tiny socks.

It had come in the mail several days ago, but she hadn't found the nerve to open it. Things were too perfect to risk messing up. Except she knew that if they didn't address the baby elephant in the room, she might only be allowing herself to fall deeper in love for nothing.

When she returned to the living room, Dane and Walker were huddled together on the couch, with Arden in the middle, shaking her fists up at them and wiggling excitedly like she did every time they played with her. Even her daughter had fallen for the pair.

It would be better to know now if that wasn't going to last.

Joy approached slowly, still loath to interrupt what had been the best days of her life.

Dane looked up at her and his giant smile shrank. "What do you have there?"

Walker's head whipped up and he frowned. "Is that what I think it is?"

"Your results. Yep." She held the envelope out to them, but Dane recoiled as if it was the most poisonous snake in the world.

"I don't want that." He turned his head and stared out the window a moment before he returned his focus to Arden, this time with a profound sadness in his gaze instead of the bliss that had been there only moments before.

He might not, but Walker…

He had a right to know if that's what he needed.

Joy Ride

Walker settled Arden in Dane's arms, then paused before extending his hand. Joy put the envelope in his and held her breath.

Instead of sliding his finger beneath the seal on the back, he put both fists on the top of the legal-sized paper, then ripped the thing in half with a *shrrp* that sliced through the room. Even Arden stared as if she knew how momentous the occasion was.

Walker stacked the pieces, then ripped them again and again until the test results were completely shredded. He sprinkled them all over the floor and dusted his hands. "It doesn't matter, Joy. Arden is ours. All of ours. I'm sorry that I didn't understand right away how we were meant to be. You guys are my family and I don't ever plan to let you doubt it again. I'm not going anywhere, and neither are the three of you."

"You deserve this," Dane told Walker. "You're not your father and you have nothing to be ashamed of. You know that, right?"

"I'm working on it." Walker shrugged. "I'll keep doing my best."

"Thank you," Dane sighed.

"So I expect the same of you," Walker stared into Dane's eyes from a few inches away, making Joy shift as she imagined where their connection might lead. They were so intense together, they brought her along too. "We're as safe as we can be here, while Clive is locked up and Jordan and his team are working to shut down Wildfire. I'm going to give the deposition he asked for. Tell them everything I know. Even then, shit happens. You can't blame yourself if it does."

"I know." Dane winced. "But when I start to get

anxious, I'm going to need you two to calm me down. In as many creative ways as possible."

"Deal." Walker sealed his promise with a kiss. Then he looked to Joy. "How about you? Are you good now too?"

"Yeah." She nodded, unable to talk for a few moments. "I have everything I need. I'll be even better when Auntie Sevan is finished with her mission and comes home to us safe and sound."

Walker nodded. "Don't worry. She's as tough as you are, trained by Wildfire themselves. Besides, Levi and Ransom will help keep her safe."

"Mmmhmm." Joy huffed. "Did you see the way Levi looked at her? Something was going on there. I wouldn't be surprised if they do more damage than Angus."

"Now that I'm a relationship expert, I'll be happy to give them some advice," Walker boasted.

"Oh yeah?" Dane snorted. "And what would you tell them?"

"That this is worth every moment of struggling." The shit-eating grin on his face said he meant every word despite the teasing glint in his eyes. "You know, the sex, the intimacy, the unbreakable bond we share. Laughter, loving, working hard to build a new life. Even the fights, and especially our daughter. All of it."

"That's good, because I think they're in for a rough ride." Dane's mouth set in a grim slash. Joy wanted to turn it into a smile. Walker must have been on the same page.

They all were these days. Finally.

"You guys, Arden's falling asleep," Walker whispered. "We might not be able to take our motorcycles out to clear our heads while she naps, but we can still go for a joy ride together."

Joy Ride

Enough said. Joy stripped her shirt off, already heading for their bedroom. "Do I get to drive today? Because I have a lot of things I want to try out…"

Dane fist-bumped Walker as they rose together. As Walker laid Arden in her bassinet and kissed her forehead, Dane said, "Sure. I love it when you take charge. Honestly, I love everything about you."

"I love you too, both of you." Joy stepped out of her pants and stood, completely naked—bared body, heart, and soul—in front of them.

Walker grabbed Dane's hand and dragged him over to Joy. He crushed them both in a bear hug and promised them forever between kisses. "I love you too. This is everything I dreamed of yet thought I couldn't have. I'm never letting go, understand? You're mine."

"Always have been." Dane nodded.

"Well, now I'm yours, and yours, too." He unfastened his pants, prepared to prove it.

∽

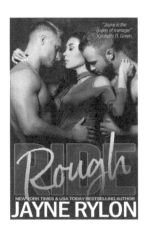

To find out what happens when Rivet, Levi, and Ransom infiltrate the Wildfire MC, read Rough Ride by clicking HERE.

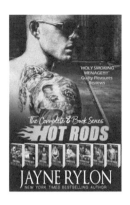

If you missed out on the Powertools: Hot Rods series, you can buy all eight books in a discounted single-volume boxset by clicking HERE.

If you'd like to start at the very beginning with the Powertools Crew, you can download a discounted boxset of the first six books HERE.

Yes, know it says complete series but I wrote a seventh book more recently and haven't gotten around to updating the boxset yet, sorry!

You can find the seventh Powertools book, More the Merrier, HERE.

CLAIM A $5 GIFT CERTIFICATE

Jayne is so sure you will love her books, she'd like you to try any one of your choosing for free. Claim your $5 gift certificate by signing up for her newsletter. You'll also learn about freebies, new releases, extras, appearances, and more!

www.jaynerylon.com/newsletter

WHAT WAS YOUR FAVORITE PART?

Did you enjoy this book? If so, please leave a review and tell your friends about it. Word of mouth and online reviews are immensely helpful and greatly appreciated.

JAYNE'S SHOP

Check out Jayne's online shop for autographed print books, direct download ebooks, reading-themed apparel up to size 5XL, mugs, tote bags, notebooks, Mr. Rylon's wood (you'll have to see it for yourself!) and more.
www.jaynerylon.com/shop

LISTEN UP!

The majority of Jayne's books are also available in audio format on Audible, Amazon and iTunes.

ABOUT THE AUTHOR

Jayne Rylon is a *New York Times* and *USA Today* bestselling author who has sold more than one million books. She has received numerous industry awards including the Romantic Times Reviewers' Choice Award for Best Indie Erotic Romance and the Swirl Award, which recognizes excellence in diverse romance. She is an Honor Roll member of the Romance Writers of America. Her stories used to begin as daydreams in seemingly endless business meetings, but now she is a full time author, who employs the skills she learned from her straight-laced corporate existence in the business of writing. She lives in Ohio with her husband, the infamous Mr. Rylon, and their cat, Frodo. When she can escape her purple office, she loves to travel the world, avoid speeding tickets in her beloved Sky, SCUBA dive, hunt Pokemon, and–of course–read.

Jayne Loves To Hear From Readers
www.jaynerylon.com
contact@jaynerylon.com
PO Box 10, Pickerington, OH 43147

- facebook.com/jaynerylon
- twitter.com/JayneRylon
- instagram.com/jaynerylon
- youtube.com/jaynerylonbooks
- bookbub.com/profile/jayne-rylon
- amazon.com/author/jaynerylon

ALSO BY JAYNE RYLON

4-EVER

A New Adult Reverse Harem Series

4-Ever Theirs

4-Ever Mine

EVER AFTER DUET

Reverse Harem Featuring Characters From The 4-Ever Series

Fourplay

Fourkeeps

POWERTOOLS: THE ORIGINAL CREW

Five Guys Who Get It On With Each Other & One Girl. Enough Said?

Kate's Crew

Morgan's Surprise

Kayla's Gift

Devon's Pair

Nailed to the Wall

Hammer it Home

More the Merrier *NEW*

POWERTOOLS: HOT RODS

Powertools Spin Off. Keep up with the Crew plus...

Seven Guys & One Girl. Enough Said?

King Cobra

Mustang Sally

Super Nova

Rebel on the Run

Swinger Style

Barracuda's Heart

Touch of Amber

Long Time Coming

POWERTOOLS: HOT RIDES

Powertools and Hot Rods Spin Off.

Menage and Motorcycles

Wild Ride

Slow Ride

Hard Ride

Joy Ride

Rough Ride

MEN IN BLUE

Hot Cops Save Women In Danger

Night is Darkest

Razor's Edge

Mistress's Master

Spread Your Wings

Wounded Hearts

Bound For You

DIVEMASTERS

Sexy SCUBA Instructors By Day, Doms On A Mega-Yacht By Night

Going Down

Going Deep

Going Hard

STANDALONE

Menage

Middleman

Nice & Naughty

Contemporary

Where There's Smoke

Report For Booty

COMPASS BROTHERS

Modern Western Family Drama Plus Lots Of Steamy Sex

Northern Exposure

Southern Comfort

Eastern Ambitions

Western Ties

COMPASS GIRLS

Daughters Of The Compass Brothers Drive Their Dads Crazy And Fall In Love

Winter's Thaw

Hope Springs

Summer Fling

Falling Softly

COMPASS BOYS

Sons Of The Compass Brothers Fall In Love

Heaven on Earth

Into the Fire

Still Waters

Light as Air

PLAY DOCTOR

Naughty Sexual Psychology Experiments Anyone?

Dream Machine

Healing Touch

RED LIGHT

A Hooker Who Loves Her Job

Complete Red Light Series Boxset

FREE - Through My Window - FREE

Star

Can't Buy Love

Free For All

PICK YOUR PLEASURES

Choose Your Own Adventure Romances!

Pick Your Pleasure

Pick Your Pleasure 2

RACING FOR LOVE

MMF Menages With Race-Car Driver Heroes

Complete Series Boxset

Driven

Shifting Gears

PARANORMALS

Vampires, Witches, And A Man Trapped In A Painting

Paranormal Double Pack Boxset

Picture Perfect

Reborn

PENTHOUSE PLEASURES

Naughty Manhattanite Neighbors Find Kinky Love

Taboo

Kinky

Sinner

Mentor

ROAMING WITH THE RYLONS

Non-fiction Travelogues about Jayne & Mr. Rylon's Adventures

Australia and New Zealand